— THE —
RAILWAY CHILDREN
— RETURN —

THE RAILWAY CHILDREN RETURN

THE STORY OF THE MOVIE

LINDA CHAPMAN

Based on a treatment by Jemma Rodgers
and screenplay by Danny Brocklehurst

HarperCollins *Children's Books*

First published in the United Kingdom by
HarperCollins *Children's Books* in 2022
HarperCollins *Children's Books* is a division of HarperCollins*Publishers* Ltd
1 London Bridge Street
London SE1 9GF

www.harpercollins.co.uk

HarperCollins*Publishers*
1st Floor, Watermarque Building, Ringsend Road
Dublin 4, Ireland

1

Written by Linda Chapman
Inspired by the Lionel Jeffries film *The Railway Children* and the characters
created by E. Nesbit
Based on a treatment by Jemma Rodgers
Screenplay by Danny Brocklehurst
Copyright © 2022 Studiocanal Limited. All rights reserved
Cover design copyright © HarperCollins*Publishers* Ltd 2022
All rights reserved

ISBN 978-0-00-851398-6

Typeset in 20/20.5pt ITC Century Std by Palimpsest Book Production Ltd, Falkirk, Stirlingshire

Printed and bound in the UK using
100% renewable electricity at CPI Group (UK) Ltd

MIX
Paper from
responsible sources
FSC® C007454

FOREWORD

This story is about the amazing courage and resilience children show when circumstances force them to grow up before their time.

The heart, humanity and hope in Edith Nesbit's novel *The Railway Children*, and Lionel Jeffries' film of the same name, inspired the idea for a sequel that would speak to the children of today and honour the legacy of the original works.

The Railway Children Return picks up the story thirty-nine years later and Bobbie, who was a child in *The Railway Children*, is now a grandmother preparing to help with the mass evacuations of children during the Second World War. In the original story, Bobbie and her siblings, Peter and Phyllis, moved to the Yorkshire countryside after their father had been falsely imprisoned for being a spy. It felt fitting therefore that Bobbie would bring her own experience and compassion to support these new 'Railway Children'.

While developing the film plot, I researched the events of the Second World War and was drawn to an account of the 1943 Battle of Bamber Bridge in Lancashire, in which black and white American servicemen fought over the US rule of racial separation. I was struck by how the townsfolk of Bamber Bridge risked their lives to protect the black US soldiers. I also discovered that hundreds of young men had signed up and served underage in the army and that many of them had died for their country as children. This became the inspiration for Abe's story.

Although *The Railway Children Return* is fictional, it was inspired by historic events and has authenticity at its very core. I hope you enjoy this heart-warming and uplifting tale, and that like the original works it pays tribute to, it will inform and delight a whole new generation of children.

JEMMA RODGERS

Producer of *The Railway Children Return*

CHAPTER ONE
1944

'Lily!' Lily heard her sister's gasp and felt her hand starting to slip away from hers. She tightened her grip, pulling Pattie closer as they pushed their way through the underpass to the stairs that led up to the train station. There were people all around them – women carrying crying toddlers, the occasional soldier in uniform, children with labels round their necks and gas masks in boxes slung round their bodies on straps. It was a hot July day and the air in the underpass was thick with the smell of sweat laced with the tang of burning fuel from the steam engines on the platforms. An old man trod heavily on one of Lily's boots. Wincing, she used her elbows to push her way through the crowd, desperately trying to keep her mum and little brother,

7

Ted, in sight while holding on to Pattie with one hand and her battered suitcase with the other.

I don't want to go. I don't want to go. The words beat through Lily's mind. *I don't care if there are bombs. The war's been going on for years and we've stayed safe here in Manchester. Why do we have to go now? It's daft. What's Mum going to do without us – without me?*

She thought back to a few nights ago, when her mum had come home from her work as a nurse and broken the news that the Germans were sending more planes with new bombs. 'You can't stay here, sweethearts. It's just not safe,' she'd said. 'I've signed the papers and you're going to be evacuated to the country in three days' time.' Lily had opened her mouth to argue but her mum had shaken her head. 'No, Lily, you have to. I simply can't risk you getting hurt.'

'But, Mum, what about you?' Pattie had asked, her brown eyes filling with tears. 'I don't want you to be hurt either.'

'Come with us, Mummy,' said Ted.

'I can't. But you're not to worry. I'll be fine,' their

mum had said. 'Hopefully it won't be for long. This war has got to be over soon.' She had smiled but Lily had heard the unhappy catch in her voice.

She'd jumped to her feet. 'We're not going. You can't make us!'

But of course grown-ups could do what they wanted and now here she was, with Pattie and Ted, about to be put on a train and sent to some place in the country far away from their home. Lily hadn't been evacuated from the city before but some of her friends from school had been sent away at the start of the war and she'd heard the stories when they'd come back. Some had got on just fine but others talked about the families who had taken them in, only giving them mashed potato to eat, making them work in the fields from dawn till dusk and scrub floors till their hands bled. One boy in her class – Alf – said he'd even had to sleep in the dog kennel!

As they headed up the concrete staircase to the platform and heard the noise of the steam trains, Lily felt a rush of indignation. She wasn't a kid any more.

She was thirteen. In a year's time she could leave school and get a job. *I'm not getting on that train*, she thought, *whatever Mum says. I'll look after Pattie and Ted and keep them safe while Mum's at work.* She opened her mouth to call to her mum and tell her but just then her mum glanced over her shoulder and, in that second, Lily saw the desperation in her eyes.

She's scared, she thought with a jolt. *She can't bear the thought of losing us. Not after losing Dad.* Lily felt a familiar lump in her throat. She swallowed hard. Her dad had died fighting in the war last year. She still missed him every day and she knew her mum did too.

Watching her mum's worried gaze raking over the crowd, she took a deep breath and waved. Her mum's face relaxed as she caught sight of them. 'You all right, Lil?'

Lily nodded, pulling Pattie through the crowd to catch up.

'Ow!' Pattie complained as Lily gripped her hand more tightly.

10

'Come *on*, Pattie,' Lily urged.

'But, Lily, I don't want to go to the country!' Pattie's face creased in a mutinous frown and her footsteps slowed even more.

'Well, we're going,' said Lily firmly. 'For Mum.'

Pattie frowned but let herself be pulled through the crowd.

They reached their mum and Ted, who were waiting at the bottom of the steps, and then they followed the crowd up the staircase, being jostled and pushed. The platform was teeming, some of the mothers were hugging, others were giving instructions and the noise was almost unbearable.

'Have you got your comics, Bert?'

'Write home soon as you can, Jim, do you hear me?'

'You look after your baby brother, Jill.'

The girls and boys were wearing coats and hats and carrying leather suitcases or haversacks. In some cases, their belongings were simply wrapped up in old potato sacks. A red-headed boy who looked about six, like Ted, was sitting on a suitcase, tears rolling down his face. A girl near to Lily dropped the bag she was carrying and it opened, spilling out a nightdress, toothbrush and her spare clothes. She burst into tears as her older sister started to shout at her. Lily felt the urge to turn and run. She didn't want to be here. *No one does*, she thought, looking around.

Teachers patrolled up and down with clipboards, checking off names and shepherding children into the carriages of the enormous dark green steam train.

'The doors are like mouths, gobbling kids up,' breathed Pattie, staring at the train.

Ted heard and his face crumpled. 'I don't want to be eaten!'

'You won't be,' said their mum quickly. 'Now, listen to me, all of you. You smile when you get there, okay? Big smiles and be polite. Say "yes, sir" and "yes, madam".'

'Mum . . .' Lily said, rolling her eyes.

'Don't "mum" me, Lily. This is important.' She frowned at Pattie who had started fidgeting with her pink dress. 'Stop messing, Pattie!'

'But I don't like it,' complained Pattie, pulling at the skirt. 'It's pink and it's got bows on it.'

'It doesn't matter if you like it or not,' said their mum. 'You have to look smart.'

'But why?' protested Pattie.

'So they choose you.'

'I hate dresses,' said Pattie, looking cross.

'Well, you're wearing it,' said their mum.

Just then a whistle blew shrilly.

'Come along now,' ordered a male teacher with very short hair, shooing them with his clipboard. 'On to the train.'

Their mum swallowed. 'Right, time to go,' she said, her voice brisk.

'I don't want to go,' said Ted, throwing his arms round her knees.

Lily saw a look of despair flit across their mum's face.

'It'll be an adventure.' She gave Lily a desperate look that clearly said *help me*. 'Tell him, Lily.'

Lily felt like her heart was being squeezed in her chest

as the rest of the children started boarding the train and the platform started emptying. 'Course it will,' she said brightly. 'Just like a holiday.'

'I want you to come on the holiday with us, Mummy,' said Ted, still clinging to her legs.

Their mum stroked his hair. 'I can't, sweetheart, but I'll write. And you write to me. Lots of letters. Lily will help you, won't you, Lil?'

The carriage doors along the train were being slammed shut. They had to get on board. Lily nodded. 'Don't worry, Mum. We'll be okay,' she said, gently disentangling Ted from their mum's legs. She bent down so her face was close to his and winked at him. 'And if the people we're with are horrible, we'll run away, won't we?' she whispered.

He smiled for a moment.

'They won't be, I'm sure,' said their mum, rubbing a tear away before Ted could see it. 'And don't you dare run away!' She kissed them all. 'Go on now.'

Lily helped Ted and Pattie up the steps.

'I love you all so much,' their mum said, her voice

14

breaking. Dumping her suitcase down, Lily put her arms round the others.

Their mum's eyes met Lily's. 'You're the parent now, Lily. Look after them. Don't let yourselves be split up. Promise?'

'Promise,' Lily whispered, feeling a heavy weight settle on her shoulders.

CHAPTER TWO

With a loud whistle and great puffs of steam, the train pulled out of the station. Lily, Pattie and Ted waved until their mother became a dot on the distant platform and then they sat down in their compartment. There were three boys on the seats opposite them, who were talking and looking at comics. They sped through Manchester, past the broken buildings that had been reduced to rubble by the German bombs, steaming past the dust and dirt and broken glass. *I'm the parent now*, Lily thought, remembering what her mum had said.

It won't be that different, she told herself, trying to stay strong. She'd felt responsible for the family ever since her dad had left. *You're the man of the house now, Lily*, he'd

16

murmured to her as she'd hugged him goodbye. *Your mum is going to be busy with her nursing. I need to know you're looking after everything else – after everyone else.*

I will, Dad, she'd promised him. *I won't let you down.*

She swallowed. She couldn't look after their mum any more, but she'd look after Pattie and Ted. Whatever it took.

As the city gave way to the sprawling suburbs of Manchester and then green fields, hills and valleys, Ted fell asleep and then Pattie started squirming beside Lily, wriggling her arms into the dress and out of the sleeves.

'What are you doing?' Lily asked in alarm.

'Taking it off,' said Pattie as if it was obvious.

'No, Pattie!' Lily hissed. 'You heard what Mum said. You've got to look smart.'

'But I don't want to look smart,' protested Pattie. 'I want to look like *me*. If the people there don't want me, then I don't want them.' She started pulling the dress over her head.

'Pattie!' exclaimed Lily, seeing the boys in the compartment looking at them and thinking her sister was about to end up sitting there in her underclothes. 'Put it back on.'

Pattie pulled the dress off. 'Shan't. Don't need to.'

Lily heaved a sigh of relief as she saw that Pattie had a short-sleeved blouse and dungarees under the smart pink dress. 'You wore two outfits?'

Pattie nodded and grinned, and after a moment Lily grinned back. Pattie was like her – neither of them liked being told what to do.

Just then Ted stirred on her lap and woke up. 'Lily, I need a wee,' he said, squirming.

'You can't,' she said. 'There's no lavvy. You'll have to hold it in.'

'But I can't!' he said. 'I'll wet me pants!'

'Ted!' Lily exclaimed. 'Why didn't you go before we left?'

He looked injured. 'I did. But now I need another.'

Pattie pulled Lily's sleeve. 'I need one too!'

Lily's heart sank. What was she going to do now?

'It's going to come out, Lily,' Ted said, wriggling even more.

'I need a wee as well,' said the boy sitting opposite her. He had glasses and a round cheeky face and his label said his name was Pox.

The boy next to him, who was called Jimmy and who had a little brother with him, groaned. 'I'm touching cloth here!'

'There are no toilets. I looked. We've got to get the grown-ups to stop the train!' said Pox.

'All right. You lot wait here,' said Lily, standing up. 'I'll find a teacher. Everyone hang on.'

Lily made her way down the swaying corridor. Every compartment she looked into was full of children but eventually she found one with just a single teacher in. His short hair was slicked back with some kind of oil and he had laid out some food on a cotton handkerchief on the seat next to him – a boiled egg, some crusty bread, an apple and a small bar of chocolate.

For a moment Lily's eyes lingered on the chocolate. They'd not had chocolate for ages now! Then she remembered why she was there.

'Please, sir,' she said, opening the door of the

compartment. 'There are lots of kids who need the toilet. Can we stop?'

The teacher looked irritated. 'No stops, I'm afraid. Everyone must wait until we get there.'

'But everyone's desperate!' protested Lily.

The teacher's frown deepened. 'Did you not hear what I just said, young lady?'

'But, sir . . .'

'No stops,' the teacher said firmly.

He turned and looked out of the window.

Lily hesitated and then shut the door. She looked around the corridor and her eyes fell on a cord with a label that said: PULL IN EMERGENCY.

A smile crossed Lily's face. She grabbed it and pulled hard.

Nothing happened for a moment and then with a squeal of brakes the train started to slow. Lily darted back to her carriage. 'The train's stopping!' she exclaimed. As the train halted, the train doors were pushed open and children spilled out down the steps. They ran for the bushes and trees. Lily helped Ted and

Pattie down the steps and stood with Ted while he peed.

'Thanks, Lily,' he said beaming at her.

'Me? It was nothing to do with me,' she said, giving him an innocent look, but then she winked.

He winked back and giggled as Pattie ran over and they climbed back on to the train.

The teacher was stomping down the corridor, his bag over his shoulder, the chocolate bar poking out of one of the pockets. 'Was that you, girl?' he demanded, glaring at Lily. 'Did you pull the emergency cord?'

Lily gave him her best innocent look. 'Who, sir? Me, sir? No, sir.'

His eyes narrowed. 'I'll find out, you know.'

'How?' Lily asked curiously.

'What?'

'How will you find out?' said Lily.

The teacher put his face so close to her that she could smell egg on his breath. 'I have eyes everywhere,' he hissed.

Lily nodded. 'If you say so, sir.' She pulled Ted's hand. 'Come on, Ted.' They headed into their carriage. Lily brushed past the teacher as they passed. 'Sorry, sir!'

He glared at her again and stomped off the train. 'Hurry up, children! Back on to the train!' he ordered snappily.

Lily shut the carriage door and held out her hand so Ted and Pattie could see the chocolate bar she'd just taken from the teacher's bag. 'Teacher's got eyes everywhere, has he?' she whispered.

They both burst out laughing.

Lily joined in. 'Here. You two share it,' she said, handing it over. She'd have loved some herself but it was a very small bar and she knew it would keep them both quiet. She contented herself with getting out the apple from her packed lunch and biting into that, sucking the juice out as Ted snuggled down on her lap. He ate the chocolate in three bites and then promptly fell asleep.

Pattie took mouse-nibbles of hers. 'Here, have some, Lily,' she said, offering the unnibbled end.

Lily shook her head. 'You're all right.'

'Go on!' Pattie insisted, breaking a square off and handing it to her.

The two sisters smiled at each other and Pattie leaned her head against Lily's shoulders. They listened to the sounds from the other carriages – shouting, singing, laughing – and watched the green fields flying by as the steam train ate up the miles, carrying them far away from their city home.

CHAPTER THREE

The July sun was warming the cobbles of Oakworth high street and Thomas felt hot in his sleeveless wool pullover as he hurried up the hill behind his mum and grandma away from the church hall. In the distance the peaks of the imposing Yorkshire mountains were silhouetted against the sky, the fields of the lower slopes neatly divided by grey-stone walls and the sheep that grazed in them looking like dots of white paint. On the higher slopes the fields gave way to scrubby moorland and bare rock.

The shops were quieter than usual. Most people were in the church hall, preparing for the arrival of the evacuees but the few people they did see on the street greeted them. Thomas's family was well known. His gran,

Roberta, had been headmistress of the village school before she'd retired and his mum, Annie, had taken over the role.

Sid, who had once been the village milkman, was sitting on a chair outside his house, watching the world go by.

He greeted them with a smile and a nod. 'Now then.'

'Afternoon, Sid,' said Thomas's gran brightly. 'Can't stop, I'm afraid. We've got to get to the station.'

'The evacuees will be here soon,' explained his mum.

'Grand day for it,' said Sid, as Gran secured her beige beret on her greying hair and hurried on.

'Are you all right?' Thomas's mum said, studying his face as he caught up with her. He nodded and they linked arms and followed Gran up the hill.

Despite Thomas's nod, his tummy felt as if it was tying itself in knots. He knew it was a good thing the evacuees were coming to stay. It was much safer for them than staying in a city. He hated the idea of anyone being hurt and scared, and he thought that living in the city with bombs falling every night must be awful – but though he wanted to do his bit for the war effort, he wasn't actually too sure he wanted an evacuee living with them. He liked it being just him and his mum and gran while his dad was away fighting Adolf Hitler and the rest of the Germans. His gran seemed very excited about the thought of having an evacuee to stay but he'd heard people in the village talking – older people and the kids at school. They said the evacuees would be dirty, that they'd have lice, that they'd steal and get into fights. Thomas didn't like fighting – he didn't like getting into any kind of trouble.

It'll be all right, he told himself, pulling his cap more firmly down on his dark blond hair. *We'll choose a little one. Younger than me.* He pictured a small boy, scared and alone. *I'll look after him*, he decided. *It'll be like having a little brother. I'll show him round, teach him what it's like to live in the country and let him play with my engine set.* For his seventh birthday his gran had given him a beautiful model train that had once belonged to her brother, Peter, who had died in the trenches in the First World War. Imagining how a poor little evacuee boy would smile when he saw it, Thomas started to feel better.

Gran reached the brow of the hill and looked back impatiently. 'Come on! Come on – hurry!'

'Gran, there's no need to rush. We'll be able to hear the train coming,' said Thomas.

His mum gave him a sideways smile. 'There's no telling her.'

'I want to be there when it arrives in the station,' said Gran.

'We will be,' said Thomas.

'Not at this speed,' huffed Gran.

Thomas and his mum rolled their eyes at each other but they both knew there was no point arguing with Gran so they hurried after her.

The little station nestled in the valley at the bottom of the hill. The solid building looked welcoming with its arched windows and red door. It was made of the same stone as the village houses, the rectangular bricks in all shades from cream to dark grey. Outside the station entrance there was a bench and half-barrels filled with plants. Thomas knew his gran loved the railway – she'd told him many stories of the adventures she'd had there with her younger brother and sister when they'd first come to Oakworth when she'd been fifteen. Just two years older than he was now.

There was no one in the ticket office and the door to the waiting room was open. Richard, the station porter, was standing beside a table covered with a checked tablecloth laid out with plates of scones and drinks. He was wearing his smart uniform and peaked cap as usual, the buttons gleaming, his dark tie neatly tied. His terrier, Monty, was sitting at his feet, gazing up hopefully.

'Well, are they coming? Have you heard from them?' Gran demanded.

Richard hastily hid something behind his back. 'No need to worry,' he said, swallowing a mouthful of food. 'I heard they're running late. There's been some kind of delay on the line.'

Monty trotted over to say hello to Thomas, who ruffled the dog's fur.

'Where's Perks?' Gran asked Richard as Thomas's

mum went to the door that led to the platform. 'I'd have thought he'd be here. He doesn't usually like to miss out on any excitement.'

Perks was Richard's grandfather. He'd been the station porter when Gran and her family had first arrived in Oakworth and had helped them out of lots of scrapes. He was retired now but she was still very good friends with him.

'Grandad can't make it; he's been caught up with important business, like,' said Richard, tapping his nose in a conspiratorial way. 'Is the church hall ready then?'

Gran nodded. 'What were you just eating, Richard?' she said, as he brushed a few crumbs off his jacket.

'Nothing,' said Richard, going red.

Gran gave him her best *tell-me-another-one* stare.

Richard shuffled his feet. 'A scone,' he admitted, sheepishly bringing his hand out from behind his back and revealing a scone with a bite out of it.

'Richard! They were freshly baked for the children!' Gran said, plucking it out of his hand.

The porter's face fell. 'I've bitten it now. You might as well let me eat it.'

'Certainly not,' said Gran tartly.

Monty grabbed it from her hand. In one bite it was gone.

Gran gasped. 'Oh!'

Thomas burst out laughing.

'The train's coming!' called Thomas's mum from the doorway to the platform. 'Quick, everyone! They're about to arrive!'

They all dashed on to the platform where the elderly station master was patrolling up and down in his smart black uniform. The train came steaming through the tunnel, hissing out great clouds of smoke as it pulled into the station, bringing with it the smell of fires on a cold evening.

Richard hurried up and down the platform. 'Oakworth! This is Oakworth!' he shouted.

Carriage doors banged open and the platform was suddenly filled with the sound of voices and crying as children scrambled out, some carrying suitcases, others carrying bags, all with gas masks in boxes and labels round their necks. *Like they're parcels*, thought Thomas. Some were wearing smart coats over dresses and shorts, with berets or caps on their head, while others were scruffier – shorts held up with string, coats with buttons missing or no coats at all. Their faces were pale and they gazed around, a few of them looking excited, but most just seemed bewildered and upset. A teacher got down too – a man with short hair and a clipboard. He started barking instructions.

Thomas's mum turned to his gran. 'Do you remember arriving here?'

His gran smiled. 'As if it was yesterday.'

Thomas saw a tall girl about his age with a beret and two long plaits helping a younger girl and a little boy off the train. Once they were safely on the platform, she took a firm hold of the boy's hand and gazed around. She looked fierce. Thomas stuck close to his mum's side. There were so many evacuees and some of the older ones looked tough and scary. As Richard and the station master started handing out scones, Thomas's mum went over to the teacher.

'Are you the headmistress here?' the teacher said.

'I am,' she replied, smiling. He didn't smile back; he just handed her a form.

'Well, these are the ones for your village. Try to keep siblings together.' Then he turned to leave.

'Wait! Is that it?' said Thomas's mum, looking taken aback. 'No other instructions?'

The teacher shrugged. 'Some of them need a damn good bath and watch out for nits. Good luck.'

Thomas saw his mum frown, but before she could say anything the teacher leaped on to the train and pulled the door shut.

'Well!' his mum said, sounding put out.

Gran blew a whistle. 'Attention, please, children!' The noise quietened. 'We've got a short walk ahead before you meet your new families. Form an orderly queue and follow Mrs Clark, who is headmistress of the school here.'

She nodded at Thomas's mum, who held up her hand and then strode out of the station like the Pied Piper, the mob of children following behind.

CHAPTER FOUR

Ted squeezed Lily's hand as they headed out of the station. 'Are we on holiday now?' he asked in a small voice.

'Soon,' she told him. 'First they've got to give us pretend parents. The people that will look after us while we're here.' She was trying hard to sound reassuring but it wasn't easy. Everything here was so different. There was just so much . . . *countryside*! Green fields stretched up the slopes of the mountains that were topped by swathes of rocky moorland. Wispy white clouds streaked across a sky that looked bluer than any sky she had ever seen before.

'The air smells strange,' said Pattie, sniffing.

'Clean,' said Lily, nodding.

33

'Bright,' said Pattie thoughtfully. 'I think I'm going to like it here.'

Lily wasn't so sure. She was used to being in streets that were hemmed in by buildings with just a little patch of sky above, and the sense of space and the vastness of the surrounding mountains was making her feel uneasy. Even the houses looked different here – a strange gold and grey stone instead of the red bricks she was used to. As they walked up the steep hill of the main street, past the little shops and houses, she saw people peering at them and heard the whispers.

'Don't they look mucky?'

'Townies.'

'Dirty vaccies.'

'Better lock tha things up now they're here.'

She wondered if the young efficient headmistress in the green jacket and brown hat had heard the comments too because she called out brightly. 'Not much further now. How about a sing-song to help us up the hill!' She started to sing a song Lily knew from school, called 'There Was an Old Man Called Michael Finnegan'.

The older woman with the beret, who was shepherding them along, joined in loudly.

Lily saw the headmistress nudge the boy who was walking beside her – a country boy not a city kid. He looked embarrassed but at another nudge he joined in too, and slowly but surely the other children also started to sing.

They sang as they passed two military trucks that were parked at the side of the street. Black American soldiers were loading supplies into the back while a white sergeant supervised. Lily had met American soldiers at home. They'd always been friendly and these were too. One paused in loading a crate to smile and lifted a hand in greeting.

To Lily's surprise, the sergeant marched up to him. 'Move it, boy!'

A look of anger crossed the soldier's face. 'Goddammit! Stop calling me that!'

'I said "move it"!' the sergeant shouted, flecks of spit flying out of his mouth.

Lily saw the soldier tense and, for a moment, she thought

he was going to argue back but then his shoulders sagged and he turned away. The sergeant smirked in a self-satisfied way. Lily felt a hot flash of anger – she hated bullies, it didn't matter whether they were grown-ups or kids. Her eyes shooting daggers at the sergeant, she hurried after the others.

The church hall was packed with people. The evacuees, all tired and hungry now, lined up in family groups while the Oakworth villagers stood at the back, commenting to each other as they assessed the children.

''E looks good and strong.'

'She looks like she could be useful round the house.'

The headmistress was standing at the side of the room with the older woman and boy. Lily guessed the three of them were related. The two women both had the same strong and capable air, and the boy was sticking so close to the younger woman that Lily thought she must be his mother.

'We should choose one; start things off, Mum,' Lily heard her say to the older woman.

36

'No – let's wait,' the older woman said, shaking her head.

The headmistress seemed to accept that and clapped her hands. 'Right, let's get going then,' she said brightly. 'Who wants to choose first?'

An older man with a flat cap and wellies on his feet stepped forward. 'I'll 'ave that one,' he said, pointing to the oldest boy.

'And I'll take 'er,' said a stout woman in a flowery green dress, pointing to one of the older girls. 'She looks good for housework.'

'I'll take 'im,' said a man, nodding at Jimmy, who had been in the train carriage with Lily and the others.

Jimmy's hand tightened on his little brother's shoulder. 'What about me brother?'

The man gave the younger boy a long, hard look. The boy scowled at him. The man shook his head. 'No, I'm not taking the little lad.'

The boy howled and both he and Jimmy looked desperately at the headmistress. To Lily's relief she shook her head. 'I'm sorry, Mr Dawlish, we really do want to keep siblings together. Could you not take both?'

Lily bit her lip. This was horrible. It was like they were animals in a market. The man grumbled but agreed to take both boys. One by one the rest of the villagers made their pick. Stepping across the expanse of floor that separated the two groups to join their new families, some of the children looked relieved, others looked terrified.

'No one's choosing us,' Pattie whispered, tugging at Lily's arm.

'We're too many.' Lily could tell no one was going to want three of them. *But we're not going to be split up*, she thought. *I won't let it happen. I promised Mum I'd keep us together.*

'Or maybe it's because *he's* wearing *that*!' hissed Pattie, nodding at Ted, who had got bored and put his gas mask on.

'Ted!' exclaimed Lily, whisking it off.

At last, everyone had been chosen and there were just the three of them left standing in front of the stage. There were only a few villagers left and they all shook their heads and turned away as the headmistress looked enquiringly at them.

'No one wants those three, Mum,' said the boy, his voice sounding loud in the now almost empty hall.

'Thomas, shush,' said the headmistress.

Lily lifted her chin and glared. *Just you try and separate us*, she thought.

The headmistress's mother was looking at the three of them thoughtfully. She murmured something to her daughter.

'We won't be able to feed three, Mum,' the headmistress said.

'We'll manage,' said the older woman softly. 'Look at them, Annie. Look at their little faces.'

Lily nudged Ted and Pattie. They seemed to understand that this was their chance to stay together and they joined her in smiling brightly at the women and boy. Lily caught Ted's hand just in time as his finger started to travel towards his nose.

'Mum, I taught city children when I was doing my

teacher training,' said the headmistress in a low voice that Lily had a feeling they weren't supposed to hear. 'Three of them will be trouble. You mark my words.'

'Nonsense,' said her mother. 'Children are children. And you said yourself, Annie, families shouldn't be split up. It'll be good for Thomas too. You told me you wished he had siblings. Well, here are three – ready-made.'

Lily saw an anxious look cross the boy's face. 'Will I have to share all my things, Gran?'

'We all have to make sacrifices,' said his gran. She beamed at the children and stepped forward. 'Right, it's decided then. The three of you shall come home with us.'

'But . . .' her daughter started to say.

'Excellent,' the older woman went on briskly, ignoring the interruption. 'We're all agreed!'

The headmistress heaved a sigh and gave in.

Lily felt a swift rush of relief. They weren't going to be split up and this family looked okay. She didn't think she'd have a problem with the boy; he struck her as being quiet and she was taller than him anyway. The headmistress seemed firm and clearly hadn't wanted to take them in, but her eyes were kind, and as for the older woman . . . Lily studied her . . . she was *unusual*. Lily didn't quite know what to make of her but she thought she might like her.

The older woman saw her looking and smiled. 'I think we need some introductions. My name is Roberta, but you may call me Bobbie. My daughter is Annie, although you will call her Mrs Clark when you're at school, and this is her son, Thomas.' Thomas lifted his hand in a shy wave. 'What are your names?' Bobbie asked.

'Lily Watts,' Lily replied.

'Pattie Watts,' Pattie said.

'Adolf!' Ted announced, his eyes sparkling with mischief.

There was a shocked silence and then they all burst out laughing.

Annie shot a *don't-say-I-didn't-warn-you* look at her mother. 'Come on then, Adolf,' she said good-humouredly, holding out her hand to Ted. 'Time to take you and your Gestapo to see your new home!'

CHAPTER FIVE

On the walk back to their house, Thomas avoided making eye contact with the evacuees. He was feeling shy and also a bit nervous of the tall girl, Lily. The little boy, Ted, was all right, and the smaller girl hadn't said much yet, but Lily seemed quite scary.

He wondered what it was going to be like having them living in his house. He didn't spend a lot of time with other children. He got on all right with most of his classmates, but he didn't have any close friends – it was hard when your mum was headmistress – so he spent most of his time on his own, either helping his mum and gran, or spying for enemy aeroplanes.

Thomas remembered his gran's words – *a ready-made family*. But did he want a new brother and two sisters?

Much as he loved hearing Gran talk about the adventures she'd had with her siblings when she'd been little, it was one thing to like the *thought* of having brothers and sisters, quite another to actually have them!

We had to take them in, he reminded himself, remembering the unhappiness on their faces as everyone else had been chosen and they'd been the last ones left. *We couldn't have let them be split up. That would have been horrid.* He imagined what it must be like for them being sent away somewhere strange. Feeling a sudden rush of sympathy, he glanced sideways and saw Pattie was staring at him. She gave him a hopeful smile. He flashed a smile back before hastily looking down at his boots again.

'Here we are,' said Gran at last. She had scooped up Ted and carried him for the last part of the walk home, giving Thomas Ted's suitcase to carry. Now she stopped in front of their house and put him down gently. 'This is our home – and yours until it's safe for you to go back to Manchester.'

The evacuees stared up at the house. Thomas imagined seeing it through their eyes. It was a rectangular stone house with two large white-painted windows either side of the front door and a row of windows on the upper floor. There was an ancient graveyard to one side. It looked slightly spooky in the twilight with some of the graves looking like tables and others leaning at odd angles. Thomas caught a mixture of alarm and fear on the other three children's faces. They all looked a bit lost, even scary Lily.

'Come on, I'll show you round,' he said, sure they would feel better when they were inside.

The house was homely: the furniture was solid, made from dark wood, and the walls were covered with faded patterned wallpaper. Rugs softened the flagstone floors and there were books, plates and ornaments on the shelves and framed photographs on the wall. His mum and gran hurried around turning the gas lamps on, which cast out a warming golden glow.

'Cocoa all round, I think,' his mum said.

'While Annie's sorting that out why don't you bring your things upstairs?' said Gran. 'I'll show you your bedroom.'

She led the way up the elegant stone staircase to a landing with bedrooms off it. Thomas and his mum had got the spare bedroom ready that morning. As Gran lit the bedroom lamp, the children stood in the doorway and looked around. It was a plain room with one single iron bed with a flowery eiderdown and a small cot bed. There was a wardrobe, a chest of drawers, a wooden chair, patterned curtains pulled shut over the windows and a faded rug over floorboards. On the mantelpiece above the fireplace were some books that Thomas had brought in from his own bedroom and on the bookshelves he'd put a pack of cards, some tin soldiers and a box of marbles.

'This will be your room,' said Gran, surveying Lily, Pattie and Ted, who were standing, bags still in their hands, smudges of dirt from the journey on their pale tired faces. Her voice softened. 'You know, I was brought here from a city – not Manchester but London – when I was a little girl. I came with my younger brother and sister. There wasn't a war on, but my father wasn't with us. We were missing him and it was a big change for us, so –' she gave them a sympathetic look – 'though it might seem hard to believe, I do know a little of how you must be feeling.'

Thomas saw the surprise on the evacuees' faces.

'Just remember your mummy has done the kindest thing a mother could do,' Gran continued. 'She's sent you out of harm's way.'

Pattie and Ted managed small smiles, but Lily's face stayed closed and tough.

'You unpack your belongings and I'll go and sort out some extra bedding,' said Gran.

She left and there was a moment's awkward silence where none of them seemed to know what to say. It was broken by the sound of his mum's footsteps on the stairs.

'Here's your cocoa,' she said, coming in with four mugs on a tray and setting it down on top of the chest of drawers. She saw their faces. 'I know there's not much space in here but we weren't expecting to take in three. We'll spread you out around the house tomorrow if you want.'

Ted gave a sudden sob and buried his head in Lily's

skirt. It was clearly all too much for the little boy. Lily squeezed her brother's shoulder and then turned to Thomas's mum, her face suddenly bright. 'I hope you don't mind me asking, Mrs Clark, but are you married?'

Thomas saw his mum blink, taken aback. 'Yes . . . why?'

'Is your husband away?' Lily asked.

'Yes, he's at war. He's a flight engineer.'

'Well, you must have a double bed then?' said Lily earnestly.

Thomas couldn't stop a smile as he saw his mum start to frown as she worked out where Lily was going with her questions. 'Well, yes . . . but why?'

'It's just . . . like you say, there's three of us and only one of you so . . .' Lily gazed at her wide-eyed as if the solution was obvious.

Thomas's mum looked shocked. 'You want my bed? But . . .'

Lily grinned, her face lighting up like a beacon. 'It's okay, Mrs Clark. I'm only messing! We'd rather be in the same room but I had you there for a moment, didn't

I?' She giggled, sounding like a kid for the first time instead of a grown-up. Ted and Pattie both joined in and Thomas saw the sudden relief in Lily's eyes as she glanced at Ted. He realised she'd just wanted to put a smile back on her little brother's face.

Thomas's mum shook her head, smiling. 'Right, cocoa, teeth and bed,' she said. 'Come on, Thomas. Leave them to settle in now.'

As Thomas was leaving, he took a last look back at Lily, who was tickling Ted to make him laugh. He'd never met a girl like her before and he wasn't quite sure how he felt about her. Once, when he'd been little, he'd come face to face with an old dog fox in the back garden. He hadn't known whether to be frightened or delighted and he felt a similar way now. One thing was certain, though – things were definitely going to be more interesting with her around!

CHAPTER SIX

'It's so dark out there,' said Pattie, sitting on the window seat and staring out as Lily unpacked their clothes and put them in the chest of drawers. 'There are no street lights. And look at the stars. They're so bright!'

Ted clambered up beside her and pressed his nose to the window. 'It's scary,' he said, his breath steaming up the window.

'Don't be soft. It's not scary,' Lily said, joining them. 'It's just the countryside.'

'I wish we were at home,' said Ted forlornly. 'I want—'

Just then there was a hooting sound and a ghostly white shape flew past their window.

Ted yelped and leaped off the window seat. 'What was that?'

There was another hoot and Ted scrambled under the bed.

'Ted, stop being daft! Come out,' said Lily.

'No, there's a monster!' quavered Ted.

'It's just an owl,' said Pattie. She looked at Lily uncertainly. 'Isn't it?'

Lily nodded. 'Yeah.' She glanced towards the bed. 'Don't worry, Ted, they only eat little –' she paused and grinned, seeing a chance to distract him from thoughts of home and their mum – *'girls.'*

Ted moaned and burrowed deeper. 'Has it gone yet?'

'It has,' said Lily. 'It's gone to chew on a baby's ear.'

Ted wailed.

Pattie frowned at Lily as if to say *cut it out* but Lily knew what she was doing. It was better Ted was scared by thoughts of mythical baby-eating owls than crying about missing their mum. She turned and stared out at the stars.

'I wonder what Mum's doing now,' Pattie said softly. 'Do you think she's avoiding the bombs?'

'I'm sure she is,' said Lily. 'The sirens will warn her when any bombs are coming and she'll be able to get inside the shelter where it'll be safe.'

'Why send us away then – if it's so safe?' asked Pattie.

Lily hesitated. 'Just in case.'

Pattie gave Lily a sideways look. 'Everyone said Dad was safe. Everyone said *he'd* be fine.'

'Pattie!' Lily hissed, putting a finger to her lips and glancing to the bed where Ted was still hiding. 'Don't talk about Dad, okay?' she whispered, feeling the familiar wrench in her heart.

There was a knock on the door and Thomas came in, his arms full of blankets and cushions. He could only just see over the top of the pile. 'Here you go,' he said. 'Gran said if we cram all the cushions together it'll make a massive big bed on the floor – it'll be really cosy.' He frowned and looked around. 'Where's Ted?'

Lily motioned downwards with her eyes.

Thomas peered under the bed. Ted squealed.

'What are you doing?' Thomas asked.

'Do . . . do owls eat children and babies, Thomas?' Ted asked shakily.

'No,' said Thomas, surprised. 'They only eat mice and rats.'

'Rats! You've got rats here as well!' cried Ted, horrified. 'Ohhhhhh, I hate this place!'

Thomas looked questioningly at Lily and Pattie. Lily gave him a *don't worry* look. But Thomas couldn't help worrying – he didn't like to see the little boy upset. He had a sudden idea and reached into his shorts' pocket.

'Really, Ted?' he said, pulling something out. 'Do you really hate *everything* here? Even sweets?'

'Sweets?' Ted's head popped out from under the bed, dust sticking to his tousled hair.

'Yeah, sweets,' said Thomas, opening his hand to show four lemon sherbets wrapped in paper. 'I've been saving them from my last sweet ration but maybe . . .' He hesitated and gave the girls a tentative look. 'Maybe we could all share them.'

Lily grinned at him. 'Now you're talking!'

Ted crawled out from under the bed. Thomas handed the lemon sherbets round and they all squished up on the cushions, a companionable silence descending as they tried to make their sweets last as long as possible.

Bobbie read them a bedtime story and then turned off the light. 'Sleep well,' she said softly, going to the door. 'My mother used to say the great thing to be is cheerful and, though it seems hard at times, it does help. I promise.' She slipped out, closing the door.

Lily was in the single bed while Pattie and Ted were sleeping on the cushions. Ted was supposed to sleep in the cot bed but he'd decided he'd rather sleep on the floor with Pattie. Lily stared into the velvety darkness of the room. It was so quiet in the country, she realised. No cars. No buses. No people outside. She wasn't used to it at all. Although she was tired, she couldn't sleep. There were too many thoughts whizzing round in her head – their mum, their old home, the new family who'd taken them in. *I wonder what Dad would think of us being here*, she thought.

She pictured their dad the last time they'd seen him – his smart uniform, his kit bag slung over his shoulder – hugging the three of them as they had clung to him, not wanting him to go. The memory stung like a stinging nettle and she had to shut her eyes tightly for a few minutes, fighting the tears.

He'll come back, sweethearts, their mum had said as they'd watched their dad walking away, waving until he reached the end of the street.

But he hadn't. Lily's throat contracted. He'd been killed. She would never forget her mum's cry of despair as she had read the telegram that had told them the news. *I hate this stupid war*, she thought passionately. *Hate it, hate it, hate it.*

'Lily?' Ted's voice came from the floor. 'I can't sleep.'

'Do you want to come in here?' she asked.

She pulled back the covers and Ted climbed in beside her. Lily wrapped her arms round him, feeling his solid, comforting warmth.

'Can I come in too?' asked Pattie in a small voice.

'Course,' said Lily.

CHAPTER SIX

A minute later and Pattie was snuggled into the single bed with them too. Lily was squashed but she didn't care. She felt better with her brother and sister beside her and, as she heard their breathing steady and Ted start to snore softly, she finally fell asleep herself.

CHAPTER SEVEN

Lily, Pattie and Ted weren't the only ones who ended up sharing a bed. Thomas couldn't stop thinking about the other three children in the house and in the end he took his torch and went to his mum's room.

She sat up in surprise as he opened the door. 'Are you all right, Tom?'

He nodded. 'I can't sleep. It's just –' he hesitated – 'odd having strange people in the house.'

His mum smiled at him. 'They're not that strange. They're just kids, like you.'

'Not really. City kids are different,' he said.

His mum pulled back the covers and he got in beside her. 'Well, tell you what,' she said as he turned on his side. 'Let's try and make them into country kids, shall we?'

He nodded. 'All right.'

They lay there in silence for a few minutes and Thomas felt himself starting to get sleepy. 'Mum,' he said. 'We've not had a letter from Dad in ages. Do you think he's still in France?'

His mum shrugged. 'I don't know, darling, but I am sure that wherever he is, he's fine.'

'When do you think he'll come home, Mum?' Thomas asked.

'Soon,' his mum whispered, stroking his hair. 'Germany is getting weaker all the time; their forces are retreating and the allied troops are winning the battle of the skies. We just need Hitler to accept it and then the fighting and bombing can be over and the soldiers like Daddy can come back.'

Thomas nodded, and thinking about his dad, wondering where he was and what he was doing, he finally fell asleep.

When Thomas woke up the next morning, it took him a moment to remember that all the events from the day before were real. He heard voices in the kitchen and sat up in bed. The evacuees! His mum was up already so Thomas hurried to his own bedroom, got dressed and went downstairs. His mum was organising Lily, Pattie and Ted into a group by the back door. 'That's it, boots on,' she said, crouching down to help Ted tie his laces.

'Thomas!' said Ted happily, waving to Thomas as if they were best friends.

Pattie beamed at him.

Thomas felt his stomach curl. The ease he'd experienced with the three children had vanished in the night and now he just felt awkward. Lily gave him a very brief smile before looking away. He wondered if she felt the same embarrassment. 'Hi,' he mumbled, blushing.

'Grab your boots too, Thomas,' said his mum, picking up a wicker basket from beside the door. 'We're going out.' She opened the door and herded them into the garden.

Thomas quickly laced his boots and caught up just as they reached the squeaking old wooden gate that led into the graveyard. It was a fresh bright morning and swallows were swooping through the sky and diving down to pick up beakfuls of mud for their nests in the old outbuildings. Silver dew laced the grass and sparkled on the pink rose heads that hung heavily on slender branches. At the base of the garden wall, poppies were just starting to open up in the first rays of the sun and beyond the gate wild rabbits hopped between the ancient graves.

'I thought we were having breakfast,' said Lily suspiciously, looking around.

'We are,' said Thomas's mum with a smile. 'But first you need to fetch it.' She led the way down the graveyard path.

'Look at all them rabbits!' exclaimed Pattie, watching the rabbits scatter, their white tails bobbing as they hopped into the safety of their burrows.

'And rabbit poo!' said Lily, pointing at the ground.

'Yuck!' said Pattie, jumping over the poo.

Thomas grinned. 'You're living in the country now,' he said. 'You'll have to get used to that.'

Ted laughed. 'I like the country! It's got poo!'

'Lots of it,' said Annie gravely. 'Rabbit poo, sheep poo . . .'

'Cow poo, horse poo,' continued Thomas, his smile broadening as he saw Ted's delighted face.

'Poo!' the little boy repeated, chuckling.

The path led into a walled sloping field with an old tractor and some rusty farm equipment. On a flat bit of ground, near the gate and the tractor, was a wooden chicken coop.

'It's a tiny house!' Pattie exclaimed, pointing. 'Who does it belong to?'

'Someone who's going to give you a good breakfast to set you up for your first day at school,' said Annie.

The evacuees swapped mystified looks. Annie nodded to Thomas and he ran over and opened the little door in the centre of the coop. White and brown hens came out, clucking loudly as they jumped down from the coop in a flurry of wings.

Ted hid behind Annie's legs and stared in astonishment as the hens started pecking at the grass. Pattie squealed in delight and even Lily smiled.

'Chickens!' said Ted.

Annie nodded. 'And where you get chickens, you get eggs. Now, who's collected eggs before?'

The evacuees stared at her as if she'd just asked who'd been to the moon before.

'Don't you have hens in the city?' Thomas asked them curiously.

'Only in the oven,' said Lily with a laugh.

Thomas's mum handed the basket to him. 'Go on then, Thomas. Show them how to get their breakfast.'

Thomas walked towards the chicken coop. 'Come on,' he said, looking round and seeing that the others were hanging back. 'What are you waiting for?'

'Will . . . will they peck us?' Pattie asked nervously.

'Peck you? No, they're more scared of you than you are of them,' said Thomas, enjoying being the one who knew what to do. He clapped his hands and the hens scattered. 'See!' The other three joined him at the side of the coop. 'There you go,' he said, pointing to the row of nesting boxes, each with its own little door and filled with a layer of straw. Thomas opened one of the doors.

'Can you see the egg?' The others nodded. 'You need to collect all the eggs that have been laid and put them in the basket. Be careful not to drop them, though.'

They all started to gather the eggs, picking them up from the boxes and coming back to place them in the straw at the bottom of Thomas's basket.

'They're warm,' breathed Pattie, as she carefully put two down.

'Straight from the hen's bottom!' said Thomas with a laugh.

'Yuck!' Pattie pulled a face.

'They taste really good, though, when they're fresh,' said Thomas.

'We haven't had real eggs in ages,' said Lily. 'Back home we just get given dried egg powder.'

'Well, that's another thing you'll have to get used to, living in the country,' said Thomas. 'Fresh eggs every day.'

'I think I can definitely get used to that!' said Pattie.

They finished collecting the eggs and left the coop.

'Looks like we'll be having a good breakfast today,'

Thomas said, showing his mum the contents of the basket.

Ted was looking sad. 'My mummy loves eggs.'

Thomas's mum crouched down and hugged him. 'Well, when she's able to come and visit you can show her the hens and she can eat some of the eggs, just like you will be doing today before we go off to school. In the meantime, you can tell her all about it in a letter.' She pulled back and looked into his face. 'Does that sound like a plan?'

Ted nodded.

Annie straightened up and took his hand. 'Good. Now, I think we need some exercise before breakfast. Come on, let's run, shall we?'

She started to run down the hilly field with him, getting faster and faster. Pattie whooped and followed. Ted put down the basket and glanced at Lily, who was looking like she didn't quite know what to do. 'Want to join in?' he said tentatively.

'Um . . .'

'Bet I can beat you to the bottom!' he said.

Her eyes sparkled. 'Bet you bloomin' well can't!' She set off down the field and he raced after her.

'Mind the mud, children!' gasped Annie, looking round. 'It's slipp . . . eeeeee!' she shrieked as her feet slid from under her and she slapped down on her bottom.

All four children stopped and burst out laughing. Ted laughed so hard he almost fell over too. Thomas held his sides they hurt so much.

'Funny, is it?' demanded his mum.

'Yes!' cried all the children.

Annie held out her hand to Thomas. 'Well, don't just stand there. Help me up!'

He grabbed her hand but as he was heaving her up, his feet slipped too. His arms windmilled and he fell over on to his back, his mum falling down beside him. Pattie tried to run over to help them but she just ended up falling on top of Thomas.

Lily and Ted burst into fresh peals of laughter.

Ted hopped from side to side. 'I'm about to wet my pants!'

'You're always about to wet your pants, Ted!' Lily

exclaimed, laughing even harder and laughing along with her, Thomas felt the final shreds of his earlier embarrassment and awkwardness vanish like the dew in the summer sun.

CHAPTER EIGHT

After breakfast with faces washed, hair brushed and rebraided and clean underwear on, the evacuees set off with Thomas for school. Annie had gone on ahead of them to open the building.

As they reached the main street, they heard voices. Evacuees and village kids were coming out of houses and streaming along the cobbled street. Some of them were mingling and mixing, others were staying in groups of either village kids or evacuees. The two groups sent wary looks at each other.

'Dirty vaccies,' she heard one boy – a boy with ginger hair and hard eyes – mutter as she passed.

Ignoring him, Lily spotted Pox and Jimmy and

Jimmy's little brother from the train. She fell into step beside them. 'How are your families then?'

'Rotten,' said Pox with a groan. 'The grandad picks his toes.'

'Count yourself lucky,' Jimmy told him. 'The mum where I am never stops farting.'

They all pulled faces.

'What are yours like?' Pox asked Lily.

She hesitated then smiled. 'They'll do, I suppose.'

The children all gathered in the school hall for assembly. There was a teacher – Mrs Eckersley – and Annie, who did some teaching as well as being the headmistress. Now she stood on the stage, looking every inch a strict headteacher. 'Before your lessons start, we need to talk about rules.'

'Boring,' Pox said under his breath.

Lily grinned at him. Beside her Thomas shuffled uncomfortably. She could tell he didn't like the fact they were talking when they should be quiet.

'Now, I'm absolutely sure you're all good kids and you were exceedingly well behaved in your previous schools . . .' Annie raised her eyebrows and a laugh ran round the room. 'But I want to be clear that here at St Mark's we have certain rules that we will not tolerate being broken. One –' she ticked the rules off on her fingers – 'respect for our elders. Two – honesty at all times. Three – no fighting, no spitting, no biting. And four – most important of all – comradeship. We are in this terrible war because some people cannot get along with their fellow men. That will not happen in this school! Okay?' Lily saw her gaze linger on a boy. It was the same boy with ginger hair who Lily had noticed in the street. He was just reaching out to flick the head of an evacuee who was standing in front of him. Catching Annie's gaze, he reluctantly pulled his hand back.

'Who's that boy?' Lily whispered to Thomas.

'Georgie Duckworth,' he whispered back, glancing nervously up at his mum. 'Shh, though. We're not supposed to talk in assembly.'

Glancing over at Georgie Duckworth again Lily saw him looking at his friends and holding his nose as if the evacuees in front of him smelled. Her eyes narrowed. She had the feeling that she and Georgie were not going to get on at all!

It was strange being in a new school with new people but Lily liked being able to write to her mum. Their teacher said they could write letters home and at breaktime she and Pattie were allowed to go and help Ted write a letter too. 'We won't put anything bad,' Lily told Ted. 'We don't want Mum to worry.'

'There isn't anything bad anyway,' said Pattie cheerfully. 'I just had lots of nice things to tell her.'

'I want to say about the owls,' said Ted solemnly. 'Write that down for me, Lily.' He started to dictate. 'Dear Mum. There are owls here that eat people and babies. But I like the chickens. Please will you come and see me? If you do, Annie says you can have an egg.' He looked at Lily, who was scribbling his words down. 'Did you write all that?' he checked.

'Just finishing,' said Lily, adding at the bottom: *PS Don't worry, Mum. He's fine!*

When school ended, it was a relief to be released from the hot stale classroom into the fresh air. 'Let's play something!' said Pattie when they got back to the house. She ran through the garden to the graveyard.

They all followed her.

'Let's play tick!' shouted Lily, running round a table-like grave. 'Bagsy not be on.'

'I'll be on!' Pattie whooped and chased after her. Ted darted behind one of the other gravestones.

'What's up, Thomas?' called Lily, noticing that Thomas was still standing by the gate, twisting his cap in his hands. 'Why are you standing there like a lemon?'

'I don't think we should,' said Thomas, nodding uncomfortably at the graves.

'They're dead!' said Lily.

'I know but it's still disrespectful,' said Thomas.

Lily grinned. 'Tell you what, if any of them complain we'll stop, okay?'

Thomas put his cap on his head and joined in but Lily could tell he was reluctant and it made the game less fun. 'Should we do something else?' she said after a bit.

'We could go down the railway,' Thomas suggested.

'Ooh, let's!' said Pattie excitedly.

'Yeah! Yeah!' said Ted, jumping up and down. 'I want to see the trains!'

'Come on then. This is the quickest way,' said Thomas, heading over to a wall at the edge of the graveyard and climbing over it.

'These stones look like teeth,' said Pattie, inspecting the top of the wall as she followed him. 'Big sharp teeth.'

Lily pointed to a clump of moss that was blanketing the stones. 'This wall needs to go to the dentist!' she said, grinning.

The ground sloped steeply away. In the valley below Lily could see the station buildings and the railway line with its telegraph poles, wires, sleepers and signals and far away, in the distance, there was a great big bridge with arches. They hurried down the slope. The turf was short, broken by outcroppings of grey rocks. Clouds streaked the blue sky and yellow butterflies danced over the sun-baked grass. Ted and Pattie chased after them. Lily felt an unfamiliar sensation fizzing through her and suddenly realised she felt safe here on this sunny hillside – safe and happy. Well, as happy as she could be without their mum.

'So where's your dad?' she asked Thomas as the two of them walked on ahead of Pattie and Ted.

'I'm not sure. France, I think,' said Thomas. 'He's air force so they move around a lot. How about yours? Where's he?'

Lily hesitated. She didn't like talking about her dad – it upset her and the others – and she also didn't want Thomas to hear their dad had died in case it made him worry more about his own dad. She shrugged. 'I don't know,' she lied. 'But he's killing Germans. I know that much.'

To her relief Thomas accepted it. 'What's Manchester like then?'

'Manchester?' Lily smiled and motioned around at the

countryside. 'You see all this? Well, Manchester's the total opposite.'

'Like, how?' said Thomas.

Lily stopped. 'Close your eyes.'

Thomas gave her a suspicious look.

'Go on,' she said. 'I won't do nothing.'

He did so.

'Okay, now imagine grey skies,' she told him. 'The air's dirty, factories pumping out fumes. The houses are all in rows; we haven't got gardens, only parks, and they're all broken so we don't go in them. Bits are bombed and some of the houses haven't got windows any more.'

Thomas opened his eyes. 'Did you see it? Bombs dropping, I mean?'

Lily nodded.

'It must have been proper scary,' said Thomas, looking impressed.

Lily shrugged. 'It was all right. You get used to it. They do an air-raid siren when the planes are coming and you hide in the Anderson shelter. There are lots of people in there – the whole street and more. You wait and you wait and then *BOOM*. And if you're still alive after the noise has gone and you hear the all-clear siren, well, you know you've survived.' She attempted to make light of it, trying not to think about the fear that coursed through the shelter, the kids sobbing, the women praying silently or sitting there with fear etched on their faces.

Thomas looked horrified. 'It's no wonder they sent you all here.'

They walked on in a companionable silence and reached the bottom of the slope where a dry-stone wall separated them from a railway junkyard full of old carriages and things that had once been used on the trains – broken trolleys, old benches, containers, carriages and railings. Lily turned round to see Pattie and Ted running down the last bit of the steep slope. As she put out her arms to catch them, she felt something small and hard hit her shoulder and then her head. Two conkers fell to the ground.

'Slum kids!' yelled a voice. 'Get 'em!'

The next minute they were being bombarded by conkers.

Thomas gasped. 'It's Georgie Duckworth and his mates! Quick!'

They scrambled over the wall and into the junkyard while conkers pelted them. 'Ow!' burst out Ted as one hit his face. He started to cry and Lily felt a surge of fury.

She stopped and turned but Thomas grabbed her arm and pulled her behind an old carriage. 'No, Lily. There'll be loads of them!' He started to hurry along a narrow drainage ditch. 'This way!'

Some of the gang were sitting on top of a transport container. They threw pieces of coal at Lily and the others. She felt anger pounding through her as she pulled Ted, now sobbing, along. Stupid bullies. She wanted to kill them. But she didn't want Pattie and Ted to be hurt.

'Where are we going?' asked Pattie as Thomas darted to the left, leading the way down a corridor of discarded train carriages.

'My secret hideout,' Thomas hissed.

'Hideout?' echoed Ted, his tears stopping.

Thomas nodded. 'This way.'

He dashed into a broken-down carriage hidden behind lots of old junk. They all climbed in after him.

'Well,' he said, 'what do you think?'

'Wooooowwwww!' breathed Ted, his eyes on stalks as he looked around. There was a self-standing steering wheel in the middle of the carriage, a little coal burner with a dented pan, a couple of mugs and a tin bowl, faded cushions to sit on, some blankets on a bench and a threadbare rug. There was also a pile of old comics as well as some sweets on the side and a pair of brown binoculars.

'I love it!' said Pattie in delight. 'It's like a little house. Can I live in here, please?'

Thomas grinned. 'Maybe not live in here but you can have a sweet if you want,' he said, looking at the pile of mint humbugs.

They all nodded eagerly. 'Just one each,' he said. 'That way there'll be some left next time we come here.'

'What do you do in here all on your own?' said Lily curiously as they sucked the humbugs.

'I keep watch,' said Thomas. 'But you mustn't tell anyone. No one knows anything about it.'

'We won't say a word,' promised Pattie.

Lily was frowning. 'Keep watch for what?'

Thomas picked up the binoculars proudly. 'Suspicious enemy activity,' he announced in an important voice.

'What does *that* mean?' said Ted.

'I keep a lookout, patrol the area for anyone who seems strange.' Thomas handed Lily the binoculars. 'I'm part of the war effort, see. I watch for spies or people planting bombs or trying to bring down planes.'

Lily shot him a dubious look. 'Have you ever actually seen anything suspicious?' She lifted the binoculars to her eyes and started scanning the railway and surroundings through the carriage windows.

'Well, there was a man. About a week ago. I think he was Russian. He had a strange accent.'

Lily flashed a grin at him. *'You're* the one who's got a strange accent.'

'No, that's you!' Thomas retorted.

They both laughed.

'Anyway,' Thomas went on, 'I followed the man. He was walking around the village like he didn't know where he was going so I told the police and they went and questioned him.'

Pattie gazed up at him. 'Was he really a spy?' she breathed.

'Well, actually I'm not totally sure,' Thomas admitted honestly. 'But he's gone now and I reckon that's all cos of me keeping watch. The police wanted to give me a medal but I said no. I was just doing my bit for the war effort.'

Pattie and Ted looked impressed. Lily smiled inwardly; she didn't quite believe Thomas but she decided not to call him out. It had been good of him to bring them to his secret place. She could see it was special to him. She scanned the junkyard with the binoculars and spotted a group of kids searching among the carriages. Her mouth tightened. They were the lads who'd been throwing conkers at them. One with ginger hair was saying something to another.

'It's them kids that pelted us,' she said. 'Is that Georgie their leader?'

Thomas nodded. 'He's famous for his nostril-stretching. No one messes with Georgie Duckworth.'

'Oh, really?' said Lily. She lowered the binoculars. 'Right, you wait here. And, Ted, you stay with Thomas, okay?'

Ted nodded.

'Pattie, you come with me,' said Lily.

Pattie leaped to her feet, her brown eyes gleaming. 'Ooh, good!'

'Where are you going?' said Thomas anxiously.

Lily grinned and handed him the binoculars. 'You like watching – well, watch and see!'

Lily and Pattie had a whispered conversation and then crept out of the hideout and along the railway. They could hear the village boys searching for them. Once they were safely away from Thomas and Ted, Lily nodded at Pattie, who dashed out into the open, shouting. Lily quickly doubled back round the side of the carriages.

'Come on then, turd breath!' Pattie yelled. 'I can smell you from here.'

The boys started pelting her with conkers again.

Pattie dodged the onslaught. 'Is that the best you've got? Pathetic!'

'Dirty vaccies!' shouted one of the boys.

'You're the ones who reek!' shouted another. 'Bet you've got nits!'

'We don't want kids like you here!' yelled Georgie Duckworth. 'Go home!'

Pattie dodged the next round of conkers. 'Sissies!' she goaded. 'You can't even throw!'

At that moment, Lily, who had been sneaking up behind Georgie, leaped out and flung herself on to his back.

He roared in shock. 'What the . . .?' He turned and saw who it was. 'Right then, you've asked for it, gutter girl!'

They tussled. Georgie tried to throw Lily off his back but her arms were strong and her legs gripped him tightly. As he threw himself to one side, she managed to get her feet up behind his knees. She kicked hard and with a shout he buckled to the ground. Quick as a flash, she twisted free and caught him in a headlock, her fingers jabbing up his nose.

'Nostril-stretch, Georgie?'

He howled in pain and rage. With a grin, Lily pushed him away and wiped her fingers on the grass while Georgie rolled around clutching his nose. She folded her arms and looked down at him. 'If you know what's good for you, you'll leave me and the others alone from now on,' she said. 'Understand?'

'Aye,' he mumbled.

Grinning triumphantly, Lily stepped over him. 'Why don't you just bog off, the lot of yous!' she shouted to the boys as she reached Pattie.

Georgie scrambled to his feet and, motioning to his gang, he skulked away.

As Lily and Pattie reached the hideout, Thomas and Ted emerged.

'You were amazing,' said Thomas, his eyes on stalks.

Lily shrugged and tried not to look too smug. 'I hate bullies,' she said.

CHAPTER NINE

THWACK! Annie took the big lump of squishy dough out of the crock and threw it on to the table. 'You've got to treat dough badly to make bread. Really beat it up.' The children were watching her, Ted standing on a wooden stool so he could reach the table. They were all wearing aprons. Annie had got them out after tea and told them they were going to learn how to make bread.

'But I'm a boy,' Ted had protested. 'Boys don't cook.'

'Well, they should!' Bobbie had said tartly, overhearing. 'And just because girls cook, doesn't mean they shouldn't do anything else, does it?' she said with a look at Lily and Pattie, who grinned at her.

'Definitely not!' said Lily, and Bobbie had given her a pleased nod.

'Cooking's fun,' Thomas told Ted. 'Particularly making bread. You get to hit it really hard.'

'You try, Pattie,' Annie encouraged now.

Pattie hit the dough lightly with her fist.

'Harder than that!' encouraged Annie.

'She means like this!' said Ted, walloping Pattie's bum.

'Oi!' Pattie shouted indignantly. Giggling, Ted scrambled down from the stool and ran off round the kitchen. Pattie chased after him. 'I'll get you, Ted!'

'Children! Children!' said Annie, but she was laughing. She shook her head at Lily. 'Here, Lily. You have a go. You're strong.'

'She really is,' said Thomas with an admiring glance at Lily.

Lily stepped forward. Just then the doorbell rang.

'Won't be a minute!' Annie called to whoever it was. She dusted her hands on her apron. 'Go on, Lily. Beat it up while I'm gone!'

Lily thumped the dough, her eyes sparkling. She'd never made bread before. It was really fun!

'Punch! Punch!' encouraged Annie as she left the kitchen and headed for the front door.

Lily picked the dough up with one hand and punched it so hard with the other that a chunk broke off and flew through the air, slapping straight into Pattie, who squealed. The others burst out laughing.

Bending down, Pattie grabbed the dough off the floor, tore a chunk away and chucked it at Lily.

'Stop it! It'll make Mum cross!' said Thomas in alarm.

Lily ignored him and threw another chunk back at Pattie, but this time Pattie was ready. She dodged out of the way and it hit Ted.

He yelled and charged furiously across the room with his head down. Barrelling into Lily's legs he knocked her over. Picking some dough off the floor, Lily plopped it on to his head. They both started to laugh.

'You've got to stop!' said Thomas, looking horrified but also thrilled.

'Really?' said Pattie mischievously. Grabbing a handful of flour from the pot on the table she chucked it at him. He spluttered as it hit his face and hair.

'Right, that's it!' he said, grabbing the dough still on the table and starting to pelt her with it.

They were all yelling and dough was flying around when Annie came storming back into the kitchen. 'What on *earth* is going on in here, children? Stop it!' she shouted at the top of her voice.

They froze, the uproar stopping instantly.

Annie's eyes were blazing and she swept her hand around the kitchen. 'Clean this mess up right away!'

Lily noticed a piece of cream paper with typing on and the Post Office crest clutched in Annie's fingers. *A telegram.* Her heart plummeted like a stone as she remembered the telegram that had told her mum that Dad had been killed. In her experience telegrams never brought good news. As Annie marched out of the kitchen, Lily scrambled to her feet.

'Come on, do as she says,' she urged the others. 'Clear up.'

But just then Annie doubled back. 'In fact, no!' she yelled, her face pale, her eyes glittering. 'Get out of my sight! Go! NOW!'

Thomas pulled the back door and ran outside. Annie sank down into a chair and put her face in her hands. Pattie and Ted looked uncertainly at Lily. 'Come on,' she whispered to them. 'Out.'

She shepherded them out of the kitchen. As Pattie and Ted ran to join Thomas, who was going through the gate into the graveyard, Lily glanced back through the window and saw Bobbie joining Annie in the kitchen. Annie handed Bobbie the telegram and started to cry.

Feeling worried, Lily made her way to join the others, who had reached the graveyard wall.

'Lily is a slowcoach! Lily is a slowcoach!' teased Ted.

Lily glanced at Thomas, wondering if he had noticed the telegram but he didn't look particularly worried. 'My mum was really mad, wasn't she?' he said as he climbed over the wall.

'She was dead scary,' Pattie agreed, following him.

'She can be at times,' said Thomas. 'She is a headteacher after all.'

'And we did make a mess,' said Ted solemnly. 'We were naughty.'

Thomas nodded.

'How long shall we stay out for?' Pattie asked him.

Thomas grinned. 'About three weeks?'

Lily swallowed as the other two giggled. It was obvious that Thomas hadn't seen the telegram in his mum's hand. Should she tell him? *No*, she thought quickly. *It's not like I know what it said and his mum'll tell him if it's something bad*. Thomas gave her a puzzled look, and she realised he was wondering why she wasn't laughing along with them. She forced a smile on her face despite the foreboding that was running down her spine.

'Let's play a game,' said Pattie as they walked down the hill towards the station.

'Hide-and-seek?' suggested Thomas.

They all nodded. Trying to act normally, Lily joined in.

'Okay, well, it's starting to get dark, so we'd better have some rules,' said Thomas. 'You can hide anywhere around the station but no further. Who's on?'

'Bagsy not me!' said Pattie.

'I'll find,' said Lily.

'Round here we say "seek",' Thomas told her.

'Fine. Then *I'll seek*,' Lily copied his accent to make him and the others laugh. 'Go on,' she said, shooing them away. 'I'm counting to ten.'

'Not ten, Lily!' protested Pattie. 'We'll never get anywhere. Twenty.'

'All right. Twenty,' said Lily. She turned away and covered her eyes with her hands, starting to count out loud. 'One, two, three . . .' She counted slowly to twenty and then turned round. 'Coming – ready or not!' Her eyes scanned the junkyard and the station buildings beyond. Where had they all gone?

She climbed over the wall, spotting a rail shed near the edge of the track. Maybe one of them had gone in there? Or what about the goods office near the station building? Or . . . her gaze swept over the junkyard . . . the hideout!

She had just started to head towards the hideout when she heard a piercing shriek.

Fear stabbed through her like a knife.

Pattie!

CHAPTER TEN

From his hiding place behind a carriage Thomas also heard Pattie's terrified scream. His first thought was that Georgie and his gang had come back and somehow caught her. Ignoring the fear that spiralled through him at the thought of taking on the other boys, who were all really tough, he dashed out of the carriage. He had to help her. But then he saw Pattie sprinting away from the hideout.

'Run! Run!' she shrieked. 'There's a man in the hideout!'

She raced past Lily like a hare being chased by dogs.

Thomas saw Lily's mouth drop open. 'What's going on?' he demanded.

'No idea!' said Lily, mystified. 'She's yelling about someone in the hideout. Where's Ted?'

They stared at each other in alarm and both started shouting. 'Ted!'

'TED!'

Pattie stopped by the rail shed. 'Come on!' she begged, almost crying in panic as she beckoned to them.

'Pattie! Wait!' Lily bounded over to her. 'We can't go yet. We haven't got Ted.'

Pattie's eyes widened in alarm. 'Where is he?'

'Still hiding, I think.'

Thomas joined them. Pattie didn't seem to be the kind of girl who scared easily but now she looked terrified. 'We've got to get out of here!' she pleaded. 'There's someone in the hideout. A soldier! I saw his uniform. I think he's a German!'

Lily scanned her sister's face. 'Pattie, are you making this up?'

Pattie stamped her foot. 'Do I *look* like I'm making it up?' She pushed past Lily and started yelling. 'Ted! Stop messing! Come out, will you? Game's over! Come—'

'Wait, Pattie,' interrupted Thomas. 'Are you serious? You saw someone in my hideout?'

'Yes!' insisted Pattie.

'But he didn't hurt you?' Lily checked.

Pattie shook her head. 'He was lying down, asleep. Under the blankets on the bench.'

Thomas looked quickly at Lily. 'We should get adults.'

'No,' said Lily, her eyes lighting up with excitement. 'If he's an enemy we should trap him.'

'Trap him! But he's a grown-up!' Thomas said, shocked.

'So?' Lily lifted her chin. 'There's four of us and only one of him.'

Thomas felt admiration swell inside him. She was the bravest girl – the bravest *person* – he'd ever met.

'I'm not going in there,' said Pattie, shaking her head and making her plaits swing. 'No way.'

Thomas drew in a breath, feeling a sudden urge to impress Lily. 'I will,' he declared.

Lily rewarded him with a delighted smile and he suddenly felt like he'd grown a couple of inches. 'Should we go now?' To his relief his voice didn't shake.

'In a minute, but first we need weapons,' Lily instructed. 'Bits of metal, large sticks . . .'

'This is not a good idea,' said Pattie anxiously.

Lily ignored her. 'You two get the weapons. I'll find Ted and make sure he stays somewhere safe!'

Pattie's mouth set in a mutinous line but she went with Thomas and they started gathering the best weapons they could find – a rusty scaffolding bar, a shovel with a bent handle, a stick. Pattie even picked up a sink plunger with a large rubber end.

Meanwhile, Lily walked round the railway shed, calling Ted's name, promising sweets if he came out. Thomas saw Ted appear, poking his head round the shed door. He watched as Lily ran over to him and talked quickly, pointing to the hideout. He saw Ted's forehead furrow into a frown as Lily motioned for him to go back into the shed. Ted argued for a moment and then turned and stomped inside.

Lily hurried back to them. 'I told him to stay in there while we go and find the German. Right, are you two ready?'

They both nodded. Lily took the scaffolding bar from Thomas and led the way back to the hideout.

'What if the soldier's got a gun, Lily?' Pattie hissed.

Lily put a finger to her lips and mimed *shh!* 'I'll go first,' she whispered. 'You wait here, Pattie.'

'But . . .'

'You can whack him if he comes out,' said Lily, as if she was offering her a treat.

Pattie nodded and squared her shoulders. 'Okay!'

'Thomas, you come with me.'

Thomas's mouth felt as dry as sandpaper as he crept after Lily towards the hideout. What if it really was a German? And what if he really did have a gun?

They reached the doorway. 'If he makes a run for it, then hit him hard as you can!' Lily breathed. 'Got it?'

'Got it,' said Thomas, his heart beating wildly.

They edged into the hideout. A large pile of blankets was lying on the bench. Lily raised her iron bar in the air, holding it with both hands, then she nodded at Thomas.

Gulping, he stepped forward and pulled the blankets back with a quick jerk . . .

They fell to the floor. The bench was empty.

Lily and Thomas sagged, the air rushing out of them. 'There's no one here,' said Lily, lowering her bar.

'Pattie must have imagined it,' said Thomas, feeling both relieved and disappointed.

'I'll kill her,' said Lily, shaking her head. She caught his eye and he felt a connection surge between them. 'You're brave,' she said suddenly.

Thomas felt a rush of embarrassment and looked down, hoping Lily wouldn't notice he had started to blush. Luckily, she was already heading out to find Pattie and Ted. Thomas picked the blankets up and put them back on the bench but as he lifted them he noticed something. All the sweets had been eaten and the wrappers were now scrunched up on the floor. *Someone* has *been here*, he realised with a jolt of alarm. *Pattie was right.*

CHAPTER ELEVEN

Thomas hurried after Lily and told her and Pattie about the sweets.

'I'm telling you for the thousandth time, there was a man there,' said Pattie as they fetched Ted and headed home in the dusky light. 'A soldier.'

'Well, he's not there now, is he?' said Lily.

A thought struck Thomas. 'Did you eat the sweets, Pattie?'

'No!' she exclaimed.

'Swear on your life,' said Lily.

'I swear on my life,' Pattie repeated.

Lily thought for a moment. 'Swear on Ted's life.'

'I swear on Ted's life!' said Pattie immediately.

'Oi! Pattie!' said Ted, thumping her.

'I did see someone, Lily, I did!' Pattie insisted.

Lily gave a nod and Thomas could tell she now believed her sister. 'In that case we should keep watch on the hideout in case he comes back,' she said.

Thomas grinned. 'You mean make a secret hideout to watch the secret hideout?'

'Exactly!' Lily declared.

As they reached the house, Thomas remembered about the dough fight and his mum's anger. She did sometimes lose her temper but he'd never seen her rage like that. He felt a rush of guilt; he knew how scarce food was. They shouldn't have wasted the dough and flour.

They went in through the back door and found his gran mopping the kitchen floor.

They stopped guiltily. She fixed them with a look. 'Do I need to remind you there's a war on? People are going hungry. We're lucky here. We have more than most but we do *not* waste food. Understand?'

They all nodded.

'You three – bed.' Gran said, looking at Lily, Ted and Pattie. 'And Thomas?' Her voice softened slightly. 'Go and see your mother.'

They walked silently up the stairs. At the top, Thomas was surprised when Lily suddenly grabbed his hand. He blinked. She squeezed his fingers and let go, hurrying after the others into their bedroom and shutting the door.

He stared at the door, puzzled. That had been odd. Taking a breath, he turned and walked to his mum's room. He really hoped she wasn't still mad. He knocked cautiously.

'Thomas?' his mum said from inside.

'Yes. It's me.'

'Come in.'

He turned the handle and went inside. His mum was sitting on the bed she and Dad shared. She looked terrible, her face was paper-white and her eyes were red. Thomas felt a rush of guilt. 'I'm sorry about the food fight,' he said, running over to her.

To his surprise she pulled him into a hug. 'Never

97

mind that now.' She kissed the top of his head. 'I love you so much.' Her voice was almost like a groan. 'You're the most precious thing in the whole wide world to me and as long as we have each other, that's all that matters.'

Thomas's surprise grew but it was nice to be hugged after everything that had happened that evening – his mum's anger, thinking they'd found a German . . .

He hugged her back. 'I love you, Mummy.'

'And I love you, Tom,' she whispered. 'More than anything.'

Hearing her sniff, he pulled back and saw that she had tears rolling down her cheeks. He felt a stab of alarm. 'What is it?'

'Nothing, darling,' she said, hugging him again. 'Nothing you need to worry about at least.'

He frowned. He'd never seen his mum like this before. Was there something she wasn't telling him?

'Are you sure?' he asked, studying her face.

'Quite sure,' she said. 'I just need a hug, that's all.'

He put his arms round her and squeezed her tight,

trying to ignore the anxiety that was scuttling spider-like down his spine.

To distract himself Thomas spent the rest of the evening and the next day coming up with a plan for spying on his hideout. As soon as school was over, he hurried the others down the hill to the junkyard. It was fun being the leader for once! He announced that they needed a den they could hide in and they quickly made one using some sheets of corrugated iron. They positioned the den so they could see both the hideout and the station platform using Thomas's telescope from home and then they gathered their weapons and piled them outside.

Crawling into the den, they took it in turns to watch the hideout through holes in the sheets of iron using the telescope. When it wasn't their turn with the telescope they played I-spy and rock-paper-scissors but though they waited and waited they didn't see anything at all until Thomas spotted his mum walking on to the station platform.

'It's my mum,' he said in surprise.

'Is she looking for us?' asked Pattie.

'No, it looks like she's going to make a phone call,' said Thomas as his mum went to the station phone, which was in a little hooded booth. Remembering the night before, he started to feel uneasy.

'Who's she ringing?' asked Pattie curiously.

'How should I know?' said Thomas sharply.

'Don't get your knickers in a twist!' retorted Pattie.

Lily elbowed her. 'Pattie, shut it.'

'I'm bored. I want to go home,' complained Ted.

'Me too. I'm cold,' said Pattie.

'In a minute,' said Thomas, seeing his gran was now walking on to the station platform. He watched as she put an arm round his mum, who was talking into the phone, reading something out from a piece of paper.

Lily took the telescope. 'Your mum looks upset,' she said, giving Thomas a worried glance.

Thomas took the telescope back and watched as his gran led his mum away. 'I can see that.' Suddenly he didn't feel like spying any more. 'Come on, let's go home.'

They all crawled out of the den. Lily took the telescope from Thomas and scanned the hideout one last time.

She gasped. 'Hell's bells! He's in there! He's looking right at us with binoculars!'

Thomas grabbed the telescope from her, his mum temporarily forgotten. 'Where?'

'In the hideout! I just saw him!' Lily cried. 'Get weapons!'

'What about me?' said Ted, as Thomas grabbed a scaffolding bar and Pattie grabbed a shovel. 'Where's my weapon?'

'I've told you. You're too little,' said Lily. 'You wait here.'

'But, Lily! What if the German comes to get me?' said Ted, looking scared.

Lily hesitated. 'Okay, come with us but stay close.'

Ted's eyes were as round as saucers. 'I will.'

They ran across the junkyard and stopped outside the den.

Thomas heard shuffling inside and fear gripped his

heart. This was actually real! Someone was actually in there! 'Shh!'

'I want to go home,' whispered Ted.

'Stay back, all of you,' hissed Lily, taking charge. 'Let me go first.'

'Be careful,' said Pattie.

Lily edged towards the door. 'Hello?' she called.

No one answered.

'We know you're in there!' she said.

Still silence. They all looked at each other.

Lily took a step closer. 'There are four of us and – I'm warning you – we're armed!'

The silence stretched on.

Lily made a decision. 'Okay,' she called bravely, 'on three I'm coming in. Don't say I didn't warn you. One . . . two . . .' She pushed the door open and charged inside. *Three!*

CHAPTER TWELVE

Lily skidded to a halt as a young, slim black soldier jumped to his feet from the bench. He was wearing a green army shirt and trousers. 'Stay back!' he commanded.

Lily frowned. She could tell from the way he looked and his voice that he was American not German, which meant he wasn't an enemy. But what was he doing in Thomas's hideout?

Thomas and Pattie joined her with Ted peeping out from behind Pattie.

'Is it just you kids?' asked the soldier anxiously.

They nodded. The soldier heaved a sigh of relief and sat back down, wincing and touching his lower right leg.

'Are you a German?' Pattie said uncertainly.

Lily shook her head. 'No, he's—'

'American,' the soldier finished. 'I'm with the army, up at the base.'

Lily felt Pattie, Thomas and Ted relax slightly, clearly thinking there wasn't anything to worry about, because the Americans were on *their* side, but she wasn't so sure. She studied the soldier. Why was he here?

'Is this your hideout?' the soldier asked.

Thomas nodded.

'Well, I'm sorry that I've been making use of it but I've got a little injury so I just needed a place to rest,' said the soldier, pulling his trouser leg up to reveal a badly swollen ankle. Above it a deep wound was bleeding.

'Blood!' breathed Ted in awe.

'Shall we call the army so they can help you?' asked Pattie.

The soldier spoke sharply. 'No! I just need to take a little rest is all.'

'It looks bad,' said Thomas in concern.

The soldier grimaced. 'Believe me, I've had worse. Thank

you all for your concern but you can go on your way now.'

None of the children moved.

'Go on,' the soldier encouraged.

Lily felt like all her senses were on red alert. Something wasn't right here. 'Why don't you want us to call the army?' she asked suspiciously. 'They could help you.'

'Well, now . . .' The soldier hesitated. 'Okay, look, I shouldn't be telling you this but . . .' He lowered his voice. 'I'm on a mission, a secret army mission. I can't talk about it but I gotta carry on so . . . so –' he eyed them firmly – 'no one can know I'm here. Understand? *No one.* There are enemy spies everywhere you look and if you tell anyone you've seen me, you're putting me and yourselves in great danger.'

Pattie caught her breath and Ted grabbed Lily's hand. 'We won't tell!' Pattie whispered.

'For all I know,' the soldier went on, *'you* could be spies.'

'We're not!' Ted burst out.

Pattie shook her head hard. 'We're really not.'

'You can trust us,' said Thomas firmly.

The soldier nodded. 'If you really wanna help me, there is something you could do. In your house maybe you have some bandages? Something for pain?'

Thomas nodded.

'You think you can get hold of that stuff without anyone knowing and bring it here?'

'You mean steal it?' Thomas faltered.

'*Borrow* it,' said the soldier.

Thomas hesitated. He'd never stolen anything in his life but this was an emergency. 'Okay, I will. My dad would want me to help you; he's a soldier too.'

'Ours is—' Pattie began.

'A soldier as well,' Lily cut in.

'Then they're both good men,' said the soldier heavily. 'Being a soldier's hard. So what are your names?'

They told him.

'Nice to meet y'all,' said the soldier, lifting his fingers to his forehead in a half salute. 'I'm Abe – Abraham.'

'Like that old American president, Abraham Lincoln?' said Pattie.

'You got it, little lady. Like Abe Lincoln. Only I'm Abe McCarthy.' Abe smiled. Pattie, Thomas and Ted smiled back and after a moment Lily joined in. She still had a feeling he wasn't telling them the whole truth but he didn't seem dangerous.

'So you promise this is going to be our secret then?' Abe said.

'We promise!' they all said.

'I think we should tell the grown-ups,' said Pattie as the children walked home, back up the steep hill, the night closing around them.

'Pattie! We can't. We promised!' said Lily.

Pattie shrugged. 'I had my fingers crossed, so my promise doesn't count.'

'I think Pattie's right,' said Thomas. 'I think we should tell my mum or gran. I don't like keeping secrets.'

Lily glared at them both. 'We tell no one!' She wasn't sure what was going on with the soldier, but she wasn't going to involve grown-ups. Abe was fighting on their side, he needed help and he didn't want them to tell anyone. That was enough for her. She saw how unhappy Thomas looked about it. *'No one,'* she repeated firmly.

'All right,' he said, sighing.

Going in through the back door, they found Bobbie sitting at the table writing a letter.

'Where on earth have you four been?' Bobbie said. 'It's very late. Go and get your pyjamas on and brush your teeth.'

They headed up the stairs. At the top Lily nudged Thomas and whispered, 'Pretend you're hungry. Get some food for Abe.'

'You do it!' whispered Thomas.

'No, they'll feed you. I'll get the pills and bandages while you keep them busy. Where's the first-aid stuff?'

Thomas nodded at his mum's room. 'In her chest of drawers.'

As Thomas went back downstairs, Lily pushed the younger two into their bedroom and then ducked into Annie's room. She ran quietly to the dark chest of drawers and started easing the stiff drawers open, hoping that Thomas was keeping both his mum and gran occupied.

The first drawer was just full of diaries and notebooks, but in the second she found a red metal first-aid tin with a white cross on the top. She quickly stuffed it under her cardigan and ran out of the room, closing the door behind her.

A little while later, after the lights had been turned off, Lily opened the bedroom window. She had a torch tied to her belt and was wearing Thomas's rucksack. Inside it she had some things from the first-aid kit and food that Thomas had managed to sneak out of the kitchen – a hunk of bread, a pickled egg wrapped in brown paper, raisins, a tin of sardines, two apples and a bottle of beer. Lily had also thought to add a razor, soap and a box of toilet paper that she'd found in a cupboard on the landing. Pattie had put in her clean handkerchief and a book about Biggles from the mantelpiece in case the soldier was bored and Ted had insisted on adding two pale grey stones with lines of silver running through them that he'd collected from outside. 'They're the best ones I've found,' he'd told Lily. Earlier that day, he'd announced he was going to start a stone collection.

'All right but no more,' she said firmly. 'The bag'll be too heavy for me to carry at this rate!'

She climbed out of the window on to the roof of the lean-to at the side of the house.

'Be careful, Lily!' pleaded Pattie.

'I'll be fine,' Lily told her.

Thomas had sneaked into their room. 'If you aren't back in thirty minutes, I'll come after you,' he said, looking worried.

'Stop fussing. I'll be back.' Lily crawled down the tiled roof before shinning down the drainpipe and dropping to the grass below.

Night had curled around the world and the sky was a cloudless inky-black lit by a tapestry of stars and a crescent moon. Deep shadows pooled round the base of the gravestones. Lily felt a shiver run across her skin but she told herself not to be daft. *The dead are dead, remember*, she thought as she ran across the graveyard and climbed over the wall, breathing in the cool air that smelled of the moors high on the hills. She scraped her leg as she clambered over. Her heart was beating fast and all her senses felt knife-sharp and alert for danger.

As she began to run down the hill, she heard something that made her stop dead. It couldn't be . . .

Her blood turned to ice as she heard the familiar horrible whining drone of a German plane's engine. A bomber!

The noise got louder and louder until she could see the shape of the plane in the night sky. It was going to fly straight over the field. What if it dropped a bomb? A wave of terror swallowed her as memories of nights in the air-raid shelter crashed into her mind. The sound of destruction overhead as the bombs fell, buildings were destroyed and people were killed.

Her breath coming in ragged gasps, she started to run, her legs going faster and faster. She tripped and fell. Barely pausing, she leaped to her feet and sprinted on towards the wall that separated the field from the junkyard. *Get to safety! Get to safety!* The single thought beat through her mind. The noise was deafening her now, filling her ears, blocking out everything else. She heard a shrill whistling sound getting closer and closer as the bomb fell and then suddenly the world exploded around her.

After that, she knew no more . . .

CHAPTER THIRTEEN

Thomas stared out of the open window, his heart thundering against his ribs as the sound of the bomb faded away and the drone of the plane grew quieter as it flew on. Lily was out there! His door opened and Pattie and Ted came running in.

'Was that a bomb?' said Pattie, her eyes terrified.

Feeling like he could hardly breathe in his panic, Thomas nodded.

'What about Lily?' Pattie burst out.

Ted started to cry.

'Shh! Shh!' Thomas said hastily as the back door opened and he saw his gran striding out, doing up her coat. She was closely followed by his mum.

'It's all right, children!' Gran exclaimed, looking up

at the window and seeing them there. 'The house is fine and the plane's gone. We're safe. I'm going to look and see where the bomb fell.'

'Mum!' protested Annie.

'Don't fuss, Annie,' said Bobbie breezily, marching off.

'Asking you to stay away from bombs is *not* fussing, Mum!' Annie shouted after her, and then with an exasperated exclamation she turned and went back inside.

Pattie pulled the window shut. 'Thomas, what if it fell on Lily?' she whispered frantically.

He gulped, his stomach squirming with worry. 'We have to tell them.'

'But Lily said not to,' said Ted in alarm. 'She won't like it if we do.'

Pattie turned on Thomas. 'I thought there weren't supposed to be any bombs here!'

'There aren't – usually. There's never been any before!' Thomas exclaimed.

Just then his door opened and his mum looked in. 'There you all are.' She frowned. 'Where's Lily?'

The truth was forming into shape on the tip of Thomas's tongue but then he saw Ted and Pattie's pleading faces. 'She's . . . she's still asleep,' he stammered, blushing to the roots of his hair as he lied.

'Yeah, we didn't wake her,' said Pattie, backing him up.

'She was tired,' said Ted, nodding hard, eyes wide.

'She must have been,' said Annie. 'I don't know how anyone could sleep through that. Thank heavens it fell in the graveyard and not on the house or station.' She gave them a relieved smile. 'Come on, I think we could all do with some cocoa after that.'

She held open the door and, exchanging worried looks, they trooped downstairs.

Lily's eyes blinked open. Where was she? She stared at the wooden roof above her and realised she was lying on the floor of a carriage – and not just any carriage. Moving her head a fraction she realised she was in Thomas's secret hideout. But why? How? Slowly at first, and then faster and faster, the memories started coming back. The sound of the enemy plane . . . running down the hill . . . the whistling of the bomb . . . the explosion . . . being knocked over the junkyard wall and then Abe picking her up and carrying her, his dark brown eyes full of concern . . . Blinking, she sat up.

'Whoa, steady there.' Abe appeared and crouched in front of her. 'How's the head?'

'Okay . . . I think,' said Lily, gingerly feeling the back of it. She had a bump like the time she'd fallen off a wall when she'd been little but she knew she'd live.

Abe held up three fingers. 'How many fingers?'

'Three,' said Lily.

Abe put one down. 'Nope.'

'Two,' said Lily, pulling a face.

Abe put another one down. 'Nope,' he said with a grin.

Lily laughed and wriggled up further.

'How's that now?' said Abe, helping her.

'Bit woozy but, yeah, I'm okay,' she said.

'I heard you scream,' said Abe. 'The bomb must have

blown you off your feet. When I found you, I picked you up and brought you back here.'

'Thanks,' she said gratefully.

They exchanged smiles. Lily noticed Thomas's rucksack lying on the floor. Abe must have taken it off her. 'I brought supplies for you.' She reached out and delved inside. 'Bandages, ointment, medicine,' she said, holding up the first-aid things. 'Food, razor, soap, loo paper and . . . ta-da! A beer!'

Abe looked astonished. 'Hey, that's real kind of you. You've thought of everything. But ain't someone gonna miss that beer?'

Lily grinned. 'I'll say I drank it and that I banged my head because I was drunk!' She pulled a drunk face. Abe laughed and they looked at each other again, for longer this time. Lily was struck by how young Abe seemed. He had to be eighteen to be a soldier but he didn't look much older than her. *He's far from his home too*, she thought with a burst of sympathy. *Even further than we are.*

Abe pulled some cotton wool out of a box. 'You've got some blood on your head,' he said, dipping the cotton wool into a bowl of water that was next to him. 'Here, stay still.' He leaned in and wiped the blood from her forehead. Lily stiffened. She'd never had a boy – not one she wasn't related to – so close to her before. Abe's face was intent as he cleaned away the blood from the small wound. Lily laughed to hide the awkwardness she was feeling.

'Don't worry about me. My mum always says I'm tough as old boots. And anyway, I'm supposed to be looking after *you*. Let's see your leg then.'

Abe pulled his trouser up but winced as it reached the wound.

'I'll be able to clean it up better if you take your trousers off,' said Lily.

It was Abe's turn to look uncomfortable.

Lily rolled her eyes. 'I have seen legs before, you know.'

He hesitated but then sat down and took off his boots and unbuttoned his trousers. He started to wriggle out of them but they got caught on his feet. 'Can you help pull?' he asked, carefully easing the right trouser leg over his swollen ankle.

Lily grabbed the end of each trouser, just like she did when she was helping Ted get undressed. 'Ready?'

He grimaced. 'As I'll ever be.'

'One . . . two . . .' She pulled hard.

Abe swore as the trousers came off and his bad leg bumped down on the floor. 'Sorry!' he said, looking horrified at himself for swearing in front of her.

Lily chuckled. 'It's okay. I've heard worse.' She inspected the wound. 'This needs sorting out. How clean is the water in that bowl?'

'Clean. I made a small fire and boiled it when I saw you were injured,' said Abe.

'Good.' Lily opened the first-aid kit and added a capful of TCP to the water. 'Now, hold still.' She used more cotton wool to bathe the wound and Abe winced.

'Sorry, I know it stings,' she said. 'But it'll help to clean the wound and stop it getting infected.' Taking the lid off a tub of antiseptic cream she dabbed some on the wound.

'How do you know how to do all this?' said Abe, impressed.

'My mum's a nurse,' Lily explained as she cleaned

away the blood. 'She taught me but I've also had to learn how to do all sorts of stuff because I've been the man of our house for the last few years.'

'How so?' said Abe curiously.

'My dad went to war so it's just been the three of us and Mum back in our home in Manchester.'

Abe looked confused. 'You don't live here then?'

Lily shook her head. 'Thomas does but me, Pattie and Ted are evacuees.'

'Evacuees?' echoed Abe.

'You know – the kids they send to the countryside so they'll be safe from bombs.' She flashed a smile. 'Only that didn't work out too well tonight, did it?'

Abe was still shaking his head at the thought of evacuees. 'So your father's away fighting then?'

Lily swallowed and looked down. She couldn't bring herself to say the truth out loud. 'Yeah.'

'It's tough.' Abe spoke quietly and she heard the pain in his voice.

She glanced at him. 'Do you have family then – fighting in the war?'

'Yeah, well . . . I *did*.' He pressed his lips together. 'My big brother.' He felt for his trousers and rummaged in one of the pockets. Pulling out a crumpled black-and-white photograph he offered it up. The soldier in the picture looked very like Abe, just a bit older.

'He didn't make it,' Abe said flatly.

Lily felt a connection surge between them. Abe might be from a different country but he had lost someone too. Did he miss his brother like she missed her dad? Did he feel like he was carrying a gaping hole around with him? 'I'm so sorry,' she said. 'What . . . what happened to him?'

Abe rubbed a hand over his short dark hair. 'He was in the Quartermasters. They landed at Omaha Beach in France, but the Germans were waiting and they shot our soldiers as they got off the boats. It was a bloodbath. My brother never stood a chance – he never even got the chance to fight.' He shut his eyes and squeezed his nose, fighting back tears.

Lily didn't say anything; she knew from bitter experience that there was nothing she could say that would help.

Abe composed himself. 'I guess you're thinking, wait a moment now – if his brother died at war, how come he was stupid enough to sign up too?'

'I wasn't thinking that,' said Lily honestly.

'Well, you should, because it's a damn good question,' said Abe bitterly.

'It's not fair, Abe,' Lily said passionately. 'Nothing about this war is. I hate it!'

'You and me both,' Abe said with feeling. 'Yes, you and me both.'

CHAPTER FOURTEEN

Lily turned over everything Abe had said in her head. 'So why *did* you sign up to fight?' she asked.

He shrugged. 'For revenge. Pure and simple.'

Lily nodded. She understood. When news of her dad's death had arrived, she'd felt like she'd wanted to go and fight someone too.

'I wanted to kill some Germans,' Abe went on. 'Because they'd killed *him*. My brave brother.' He shook his head and swallowed. 'He was only eighteen years old.'

Lily frowned. She could remember her mum talking about the battle of Omaha Beach and she was sure it hadn't happened very long ago. 'How old are you?'

'Um . . . eighteen,' said Abe.

123

Lily's frown deepened. 'But you said he was your *big* brother?'

Abe cleared his throat. 'That's right. We were born close is all.'

Lily raised her eyebrows. 'You know something – back home we have a saying: you can't kid a kidder.'

Abe faltered. 'Meaning what?'

She folded her arms and fixed him with a stern look. 'Meaning that I've told my fair share of lies and so I know one when I hear one, Abe.'

'I'm not lying!' Abe protested. 'I'm eighteen. I'm . . . I'm a soldier on a secret mission.'

'So what is this *secret mission*?' she challenged.

'I can see you don't understand the meaning of "secret"!' he said, attempting to joke.

She continued with her unimpressed stare.

'Okay, well . . .' He hesitated. 'If you must know, I'm . . . I'm a member of a special forces unit and because of that I have to get to Liverpool. That's where I was heading when I got injured. It's such a secret mission that the regular army don't even know about it, which is why I told y'all not to tell anyone. Please now, don't say anything. I'll leave and you won't see me again.'

Lily considered it. There was a chance he could be telling the truth but there was still the thing about his age. How could he and his older brother both be eighteen? Questions boiled in her brain, but looking at his pleading face she came to a decision. Whatever the truth, he was away from home and needed help. Maybe he also had a mum back at home, waiting for him, worrying about him. She, Pattie and Ted had been lucky to end up with Bobbie and Annie. He didn't have anyone.

'So you've got to get to Liverpool then?'

He nodded.

'Well, you're in luck,' she told him. 'Trains run through this station to Liverpool every day or two.'

Abe sat up straight. 'Really?'

She nodded. 'It's the same line we came on from Manchester.'

Hope dawned on Abe's face. 'Lily, do you think you could find me the time of the Liverpool trains?' he asked eagerly.

'Yeah, sure. Tomorrow. But now I'd better go home,' she said, getting to her feet. 'They'll be worried about me. I'll come back after school, okay?'

He nodded. 'Okay – and, Lily?'

She paused. 'What?'

Abe's grateful brown eyes met hers. 'Thanks.'

Back at the house, Thomas, Ted and Pattie were sitting at the kitchen table, their cocoa untouched. 'Are you not going to drink that?' asked Annie in surprise as she looked at the skin forming on top of their drinks.

They shook their heads. Thomas felt sick to his stomach. All he could think about was Lily. What if she was hurt – or worse?

His gran had just come back. He hadn't known whether to be relieved or worried when she hadn't mentioned anything about seeing Lily. She'd said that the bomb had fallen on the graveyard and that she'd met Richard, the porter, there. Richard thought the bomb must have been dropped by an enemy plane flying back to its base – trying to save fuel on its way home. Gran had seemed upset and after giving him, Pattie and Ted a hug, she had gone to bed.

Annie glanced at the staircase. 'I can't believe Lily's slept through everything. She'll be astonished when we tell her. Shall we wake her?'

'No!' the children all exclaimed.

Ted's lower lip started to tremble. Thomas was about to put his arm round him to comfort him when a pale face appeared at the window behind Annie. *Lily!* Relief hit him like a steam train and it was all he could do not to jump up with joy. Lily motioned frantically upwards.

Pattie caught her breath and Thomas realised that she'd spotted Lily too. She pinched Ted.

'Ow! What was—'

Pattie pulled Ted into a tight hug, cutting off his words. 'Don't cry, Ted!' she said loudly. 'You're all right. The bomb's gone now. Thomas, can you get his teddy from upstairs?'

Thomas leaped to his feet, realising she was giving him a chance to get out of the room to help Lily. 'All right. Back in a mo,' he said, racing up the stairs.

Once in the bedroom, he pulled the window open. 'Lily!' he hissed.

He could hear her climbing back up the drainpipe and a few minutes later he saw her as she scrambled on to the roof of the lean-to. Her face was smudged with dirt and she had a small cut on her head but otherwise he saw to his relief that she looked unhurt. 'Thank goodness you're safe!'

'Give us a hand,' she said with her usual grin.

As he helped her inside, he heard Pattie and Ted's feet on the stairs.

'I think Ted just needs to go to bed, Annie!' Pattie was saying. 'I'll settle him. Don't you worry.'

Seeing Lily, they dashed over and flung their arms round her. She hugged them tightly.

'We were so worried about you,' said Pattie.

'Did you see the bomb, Lily?' asked Ted.

'Bomb? What bomb?' Lily teased, smiling.

'It was an enormous one! It went boom!' said Ted, not realising she was joking.

'I'm really glad you weren't hurt,' said Thomas.

'Where have you been, though?' asked Pattie. 'We had to tell Annie you were asleep.'

'I've been with Abe,' said Lily. 'Listen. There's things I need to tell you about him . . .' She sat down on the window seat and told them everything – that Abe had signed up because of his brother, that he'd said he needed to get to Liverpool because he was on a secret mission. Their eyes widened.

'He's like . . . Captain America,' said Pattie, awed.

'Captain America!' whooped Ted.

Lily was about to say something but then there was a knock at the door. Thinking fast, Lily pulled her hair over her forehead to hide her cut.

Annie looked in, and seeing Lily, she smiled. 'Oh, you're awake at last! Have the others been telling you about the bomb? I can't believe you slept through it all.'

Lily shrugged as if it was no big deal. 'It's war. I'm used to it.'

Annie's expression grew puzzled. 'Lily, why are you wearing your coat?'

'Um . . . I was cold!' she said quickly.

Annie eyed her with suspicion. 'Hmm. Well, maybe you should try shutting the window then.' Lily went and closed it. 'Now, back to bed, all of you,' said Annie. Ted and Pattie took off their dressing gowns and climbed into their beds. 'Thomas, time to say goodnight.'

'Can't I stay for a bit longer?' he said, longing to ask Lily more about Abe.

His mum shook her head. 'No, you need to sleep. If you're scared, you can come in with me.'

Thomas was mortified. 'Mum! I'm not scared!'

Lily, Pattie and Ted all giggled.

'Well, maybe *you're* not, but *I* could certainly do with a hug after all the drama tonight,' said his mum. 'Come on – bed.'

Thomas went to his mum's bedroom, where they got into her double bed. Turning the light off, she kissed his head. 'I'm so glad we're all . . .' Her voice suddenly faltered. 'I'm so glad *we're* safe.'

With everything that had happened, Thomas had forgotten about seeing her crying as she made the phone call earlier but hearing her voice catch, it came flooding back. 'Mum, is everything all right?' he said, turning and looking at her.

A strange expression he couldn't read flashed across her face and then she smiled. 'Everything's fine.' She kissed his head. 'Sleep now, my darling.'

He yawned. He wasn't convinced, but he was so tired he couldn't think straight any more. *I'll ask her again tomorrow*, he thought drowsily, shutting his eyes. *And in the morning we also need to come up with a plan for how to help Abe get to Liverpool. And I need to go to the station to get a . . . a timetable . . .*

With his mum stroking his hair he fell asleep.

Thomas's dreams were full of bombs, planes and people crying out. He woke earlier than usual and went downstairs. His mum and gran were in the kitchen getting porridge ready for breakfast. 'I'm just going to the station,' he told them, lacing up his boots and putting on his cap.

'The station?' his mum said in surprise.

'Yeah. I . . . um, want to do a school project about

the trains,' he said. He saw his mum raise her eyebrows. She always knew when he was lying, but she didn't try to stop him. 'All right then. Don't be late for school, though.'

Thomas took the usual shortcut through the graveyard. The bomb had fallen at the edge of it and nearby was a scene of devastation. Graves had been blown apart and the wall destroyed. Climbing over the rubble, he suddenly realised why his gran had been so upset the night before. Her brother, Peter, had been buried in the graveyard after he'd been killed in the First World War. He ran quickly away from the mess and down the hill.

To Thomas's relief, when he got to the station, Richard the porter seemed more concerned about a battery he'd just bought than about why Thomas wanted a timetable of the trains that ran to Liverpool. 'This battery is vital to the war effort,' the porter told him as he bent over a radio receiver in the cosy station office.

'Why?'

'Because it powers this radio receiver that I need

for –' Richard looked around as if checking for spies – *'listening.'*

'Listening?' Thomas echoed.

'I'm eavesdropping on the enemy,' Richard told him importantly. 'Me and my grandad use this receiver to listen for messages, to find out what they're doing. We tell the authorities about anything we hear. It's all very hush-hush, so mind you don't go saying a word.'

'I won't,' said Thomas with a sigh, wondering exactly how many more secrets he was going to be asked to keep!

CHAPTER FIFTEEN

It was very frustrating to have to go to school that day and focus on arithmetic and history when all the children wanted was to take the train timetable to Abe. But at last the bell rang and they were free to go.

They raced to the hideout. Abe was sitting on the bench reading the Biggles book Pattie had put in the rucksack.

'We got the timetable,' Lily told him. 'Well, Thomas got it,' she added fairly.

'We're going to help you get to Liverpool,' said Ted earnestly.

'For your secret mission!' said Pattie excitedly.

Abe's face lit up. 'Let me see.'

Thomas handed the timetable over. As Abe studied it,

Lily looked around the hideout. All that was left of the food was the brown paper and empty tin of sardines, and the toothbrush and soap had clearly been used – they were on the bench next to a bowl of water – but the bottle of beer was untouched and the razor was still in its wrapping. She looked at Abe's face, realising something. Men – even eighteen-year-old men – grew beards. If he'd been hiding for a few days then surely he should be growing a beard by now. *Odd*, she thought, her inner radar once again telling her something wasn't right.

'Liver-pool,' said Abe slowly. 'Kinda peculiar name for a city.'

'It's named after the liver bird, whatever that is,' said Lily.

'Where in America are you from?' Thomas asked Abe.

'New York,' said Abe. 'Have y'all heard of it?'

They nodded.

'You've got skyscrapers there, haven't you?' said Pattie.

'We do,' said Abe.

'And cowboys?' asked Ted eagerly.

'Maybe one or two – in the subway,' said Abe with a grin.

'What's a subway?' asked Thomas.

'You know, where trains run underground?' said Abe.

'Wowwww!' said Ted, his eyes huge.

'Do you live near the Grand Canyon?' asked Pattie.

'No.' Abe started to draw a map on the wall in the dust. 'So Britain is here and right across the ocean here is the U. S. of A. This here is New York City and way over here, well, that's California, where the sun always shines, and right here –' he pointed – 'is our famous hole in the ground – the Grand Canyon.'

Lily watched him closely. While he was talking about home, his face relaxed and he looked even younger.

'Do you miss your home?' Thomas asked him.

Abe nodded ruefully. 'Like crazy,' he said.

After Lily had checked and cleaned Abe's wound, they set off home.

'Should we go through town instead of up the field?' said Thomas.

'Yes,' said Lily. She'd seen the graveyard close up the night before on her way back from the hideout and she was worried it might give Ted nightmares if they walked through it. She wondered if that was why Thomas had suggested the longer route. Probably. Thomas wasn't like anyone she'd met before, with his strange habit of always telling the truth and the way he liked to stick to rules and not get into trouble, but he was all right. In fact, more than all right. She liked him probably more than any lad she'd ever known, barring Ted and her dad, of course.

'How long will Abe stay?' Pattie asked as they walked up the steep hill. The smell of frying chips from the fish and chip shop wafted towards them and Lily's tummy grumbled.

'Just till his leg's better, then he can carry on with his mission,' said Thomas.

Hearing the sound of engines they all looked round curiously. There were hardly any vehicles in Oakworth because petrol was rationed and only people like the doctor, vet and military were allowed to use cars. Two

American Army Jeeps were pulling into the side of the street. Six white military police officers in khaki uniforms and white hats jumped out. They didn't look like they were out for a casual stroll; their faces were aggressive as they walked up to the fish and chip shop.

Lily tensed, suddenly certain that something was about to kick off.

'What's going on?' Pattie said.

They're probably just getting some chips,' Lily said reassuringly, but her unease increased as the officers slammed open the chippy door.

'Can we have some chips, Lily?' asked Ted.

Lily didn't answer. Hearing shouting from inside the chippy, she hastily pulled her brother and sister behind a wall.

Thomas ducked in with them, his face troubled.

Ted squirmed under Lily's grip. 'Lily, what are we—?'

He broke off as the officers dragged a black soldier out of the chip shop. The hot chips the soldier had been holding flew from his hand and rained down on the street as he tried to wrestle away from them.

A woman in a flowery summer dress with a red belt came running out. 'Get off him!' she cried, grabbing at one of the officer's arms.

Lily gasped as the officer shoved the woman hard into the chip-shop wall.

The black soldier yelled. 'You leave her alone!'

The officer turned and pushed him hard too, yelling into his face, 'Why are you with this lady?'

'None of your business!' the soldier retorted.

To Lily's horror the military officer punched him in the stomach. The soldier doubled over in pain.

Pattie went to run out to help but Lily grabbed her. Ted started to cry and buried his head against her. Lily put her arm round them, her mind reeling at the scene unfolding in front of her. What was happening? The US military police and the soldiers were on the same side. Why were they fighting?

'What are you doing with this lady, boy?' yelled the officer.

When the soldier didn't reply, he hit him again and then shoved him into the gutter.

'No!' Pattie cried out. Lily slammed her hand over Pattie's mouth, not wanting the officers to hear them. She had no idea what was going on, but she didn't want the officers to know they were there, watching.

The soldier lay on the ground, fighting for breath.

'Go, go, go!' the officer snarled at the woman.

Taking one last terrified look at them, the woman ran away down the street, her heels clacking on the cobbles. The military officer gave the soldier a kick and then he and the others got back into the Jeeps. Doors slammed, engines revved and then the vehicles turned and drove away, leaving the soldier lying on the floor.

'Why would they do that?' Thomas said, aghast.

Lily rarely felt completely bewildered but now she did. 'I don't know. He's one of theirs. It makes no sense.' She wondered if she should go and help the soldier but people were already coming out of the nearby houses and, as she watched, they helped him to his feet, dusting him down and seeing if he was okay.

'We should go,' said Thomas shakily.

Lily nodded. Now her shock was fading, anger was

starting to boil up inside her. How *dare* the officers treat the poor soldier like that! He hadn't done anything wrong. Being in a chip shop with a woman wasn't a crime! She pictured the scene again – six white officers and the one black soldier and frowned. Could they have been angry because the soldier was black? Back in Manchester she'd heard that the officers in charge didn't like the black soldiers mixing with white locals, but she'd never seen anything like the scene she'd just witnessed.

Why would they be so bothered by something like that? she thought in confusion. *I don't get it. I don't understand.*

CHAPTER SIXTEEN

'Lily! Lily Watts!' Mrs Eckersley's sharp voice jerked Lily to attention. She'd been staring out of the classroom window, thinking about her dad, remembering the last time she had seen him and wishing she could talk to him about why the American officers had treated their soldier so appallingly. She looked round quickly.

'Nice of you to join us, Miss Watts,' the teacher said drily. The rest of the class snickered. 'Is your mind elsewhere?'

Pox who sat on the same row as Lily grinned. 'She's staring at Jimmy Goodman's bum, miss.'

Everyone burst out laughing. Jimmy spun round from the row in front. 'Oi! Shut your cakehole!'

'That will do!' exclaimed Mrs Eckersley.

'Dreaming about home, were you, slum girl?' Georgie Duckworth, who was sitting behind Lily, goaded.

She swung round angrily. Seeing that he was leaning back in his chair, she grabbed the front chair legs and yanked them. Georgie fell backwards and landed on his backside with an outraged yell. The class erupted into a mixture of cheers and jeers.

'Lily Watts!' Mrs Eckersley said, outraged. 'Go to the headmistress straight away!'

Georgie clambered to his feet.

'You as well, Georgie Duckworth!' Mrs Eckersley snapped. 'And not a word on the way.'

Scowling at each other, Lily and Georgie made their way to Annie's study, which was near the front door. If you were sent to the head, you had to wait in the corridor outside her study in silence until she came out and saw you. Georgie slumped grumpily against one wall.

'Bet you've got skidmarks in your pants after that fall, haven't you, Georgie?' Lily mocked.

'You heard from your mum yet?' he retorted. 'She's probably dead under a bomb!'

Lily moved viper-fast, slamming him back against the wall and pulling back her fist to punch him, but suddenly she heard male voices – commanding voices, American voices. She paused as two officers came into the building, wiping their feet on the mat. Letting Georgie go, she hurried to a nearby nature table with a display of things the children had brought in and ducked down, hiding behind it so the officers didn't see her. Why were they there?

Georgie joined her. She ignored him, her attention focused on the officers. What were they doing in school?

Annie was with the officers, welcoming them into the school. Lily could only hear snippets of the conversation as they explained why they were there. She saw them show Annie a photograph.

'We'd like to do a search of the area, ma'am, including the school.'

Annie said something Lily didn't catch.

One of the officers nodded. 'We need to check if anyone has seen him . . . He's a deserter. Ran away.'

The other officer shook his head, grim-faced. 'He's a

coward. So if you see him . . .' He held up the photograph again.

Lily only just stopped herself from gasping out loud. It was a picture of Abe!

Her thoughts raced. The officers were after him. He wasn't on a secret mission – he was a deserter. *I knew he was lying to us*, she thought furiously. But even as the thought formed, she knew it didn't matter. He'd rescued her and he was her friend. She had to tell him that the officers were going to search the area. She couldn't bear to think what they'd do if they caught him. She started to creep back along the corridor.

'Where are you going?' Georgie hissed.

'None of your bloomin' business!' she hissed back.

'I'll tell,' he threatened.

'Do that and I'll drag you by your nostrils all the way to Manchester,' she said fiercely. Leaving him staring after her, she hurried to the front door. There was a clothes rack beside it where the teachers left their coats, hats and outdoor shoes. Grabbing a smart beige overcoat and beret, she thrust her arms into the sleeves, shoved the beret on her head and then, hoping she'd pass for a grown-up, she slipped out. She was about to run down the street when she spotted a black bicycle leaning against a wall. It had a basket on the front and looked like it belonged to one of the boys who delivered things from the shops. Lily hesitated but then made up her mind. It was only borrowing – she'd give it back. Running to the bike, she grabbed it and rode away, pedalling as fast as she could along the cobbled street. As she rode down the steep hill, she saw other military officers knocking on doors, photos of Abe in their hand as they asked the locals if they'd seen him.

I'm going to kill him for lying to me! Lily thought furiously.

Reaching the station, she threw the bike into a patch of long grass and then climbed over the fence into the junkyard. Leaping over the discarded equipment and machinery, she arrived at the hideout and barged inside. Abe leaped up off the bench. 'What the . . .! Hey, it's you!'

'You lied to me!' Her fury spiralled through her, exploding in a shout. 'You're not on a secret mission, are you?'

'Wait, Lily, I can explain—'

Lily didn't give him time to finish. 'There are Americans everywhere looking for you. They're saying you're a deserter!'

'It ain't true,' Abe said desperately.

'They're calling you a coward!'

'That's because they think I've failed my mission,' Abe blustered. 'They—'

'Abe!' Lily shouted. 'There is no secret mission, admit it!'

Her words echoed around the carriage. Abe looked shame-faced and hung his head.

Lily took a breath, her temper fading. 'Why are you here?' she said more quietly.

He didn't answer.

'Abe. Why. Are. You. Here?'

'I'm sorry,' Abe muttered, barely able to meet her eyes. 'I didn't mean to mislead you but I had my reasons.' He glanced at her appealingly. She gave him a nod that said *go on.*

He took a breath. 'I ran away, okay, and I don't ever

want to go back, but I'm *not* a coward. I'm not! I'm just a kid – like you. I shouldn't even be here.'

Lily frowned. 'A kid? How old are you?'

'Almost fifteen.'

She stared. 'You're *fourteen*!' She shook her head. That was only a year older than she was. 'How can you be in the army if you're just fourteen?'

Abe shrugged. 'It was real easy. They weren't turning folks away.'

Lily continued to shake her head. She couldn't take it in.

'I wanted to follow my brother,' Abe went on. 'To get revenge and make my family proud. But I'm done with it now. I've been having the worst time, so bad you can't imagine. I miss home, Lily. I miss my mom.' He looked at her pleadingly. 'You know what that feels like, don't you?'

She felt like a hand was squeezing her heart. 'Yeah – yeah, I do.' Her mind churned. What should she do? But even as the question formed, she knew the answer. She had to help Abe escape. He was fourteen – a kid like her – but to the army he was a grown man and they would punish him like a man if they found him. *I can't let that happen*, she thought. *He needs to get back to America.*

'You've got to get out of here,' she said. 'They're searching the town and soon they'll come to the station and then they might find you. It's too risky to stay.'

'But where can I go?' Abe looked panicked.

'To the house where I'm staying.' She undid the overcoat and pulled it off. 'Here put this on,' she said, handing it to him. 'And stick this on your head.' She shoved the beret at him.

Abe stared at her. 'But these are women's clothes!'

She rolled her eyes. 'And the police are going to be looking for a man. So if we dress you up as a woman we have a chance – just a small one – of getting you to the house without them noticing you, all right?'

He grinned and saluted her. 'Right you are, boss!' He did the belt up and put the beret on his head. 'Lead the way!'

CHAPTER SEVENTEEN

To Lily's relief – and more than a little astonishment – her plan worked. They got safely across the fields without being seen and there was no one in the house – Annie was at school and Bobbie was out. She hurried Abe up to Thomas's room.

'You can hide in here. There's a big cupboard behind that door, almost like a little room. There's a bench and sewing machine, games and toys. You should be safe if you stay in there.'

'I felt safer in the hideout,' said Abe, glancing around nervously.

'No. You're safest here,' said Lily, thinking of all the military police she'd seen. 'Trust me.'

Abe's eyes caught hers. 'I do.' There was a moment's

silence that he broke. 'Don't you care I ran away – that they say I'm a coward?'

'No,' said Lily honestly. 'You're no coward.'

A noise downstairs made them both look at each other in alarm.

'Someone's here,' said Lily. 'It's probably Bobbie – Thomas's gran.'

'What if she comes up here?' said Abe.

'Hopefully she won't,' said Lily. 'But stay in the cupboard and hide under this if she does.' She grabbed one of the blankets from Thomas's bed. 'And stay quiet!' she hissed.

Abe nodded and shut himself in the cupboard. Lily was about to head downstairs when she heard a car engine outside. She ran to the window, worried that it was the military police. Standing behind the curtains, she peeped out. Relief flooded through her as she saw that it wasn't a military Jeep but a sleek black car. An old man with white hair was getting out. He had a bushy moustache, a craggy face carved with wrinkles and an intelligent but kindly expression in his eyes. He was wearing a smart brown three-piece suit and was carrying a leather briefcase.

As she watched, Bobbie came out of the house and greeted him warmly, kissing him on both cheeks before starting to talk quickly, her face serious.

The old man looked equally grave as he nodded and replied.

Lily wondered if his visit was something to do with the telegram she'd seen in Annie's hand but there was no time to think about that now. The others would be home from school any minute and she had to warn them about Abe!

Creeping downstairs, she let herself out of the back door. Closing it quietly behind her, she ran through the garden. The old gentleman and Bobbie were heading inside. She waited in the shadows until she saw Thomas, Pattie and Ted coming through the gate and then she hurried to join them.

Ted frowned. 'Where have you—'

'Shh!' she said hastily as the front door opened. The old man stood there, his eyes twinkling and a huge smile on his face as he looked at Thomas.

'Hello, young man!'

'Great-Uncle Walter!' exclaimed Thomas, his face breaking into a grin. He ran over but as he reached him, he hesitated and put out his hand politely. 'It's good to see you, sir.'

'Let's have none of that, Thomas!' said his great-uncle, lifting him up and hugging him. 'My, you're getting heavy!'

'It's all the food he eats,' said Bobbie, laughing as she came out too. 'Trying to feed growing children with a war on is no laughing matter.'

'I can well imagine,' said Thomas's great-uncle. His eyes fell on Lily, Pattie and Ted. 'So, you must be the three new house guests I've heard so much about.'

'Yes, they're my friends,' Thomas said happily. 'Uncle Walter this is Lily, Pattie and the little one is Ted.'

Uncle Walter smiled at Lily. 'Ah, Lily – just like the famous Lily Pons.'

Lily had no idea what he meant. 'Um . . . okay,' she said.

'Operatic soprano,' Uncle Walter went on in his deep,

rich voice. 'Stunning, absolutely beautiful. Her face could light up the night and her—'

'Walter,' interrupted Bobbie as if afraid of what he might say.

Uncle Walter gave the children a wink. 'Or so I'm told.'

Lily decided she liked him. He didn't seem bothered by the fact they were evacuees – he was treating them as if they were normal guests.

'Right, everyone,' said Bobbie, clapping her hands, 'in you come and get cleaned up. We're going to have a special tea to celebrate Uncle Walter's arrival and I need a hand setting the table.'

Everyone piled inside and the children headed upstairs. As they reached the landing, Lily grabbed Thomas's arm. 'Before you go into your room there's something you should know.' Putting her fingers to her lips, she motioned *follow me* and led the way into Thomas's room. She knocked gently on the cupboard door and when there was no reply, she opened it. Abe was asleep on the bench, the blanket covering all of him apart from his head. She saw the shock on the other's faces.

'Lily! What's Abe doing in my bedroom?' Thomas hissed.

The story poured out. In a rushed whisper Lily told them about seeing the police at school, about sneaking out and discovering that Abe had run away, and then seeing the police scouring the town.

Thomas stared at her in anger. 'He's a deserter! And you brought him here? Are you out of your mind?'

'We have to keep him safe,' protested Lily.

'No!' exclaimed Thomas. 'We have to tell the army.'

'No, Thomas!'

'But what if they find him here?'

'It's just for a day or two, till they give up searching,' begged Lily.

'But I sleep in here. What if he's dangerous?'

'He's not! He's only *fourteen*!' The words burst out of Lily.

There was a stunned silence.

'Fourteen?' Thomas echoed. She could see it sinking

in and then he shook his head. 'I don't care, Lily. If he's a deserter, that means he's a liar and a coward! Our dads are overseas, fighting, risking their lives and he just runs away—'

'He's no coward!' Lily interrupted. 'I swear down he isn't. When the bomb fell, he came out and got me. We can't give him up. It's not just because he's a kid like us – think about what those officers did to that soldier last night.'

It was clear from Thomas's face that he remembered it well. 'But what if they catch us hiding him, Lily?' he said, his voice quietening. 'What if we all end up in jail?'

The cupboard door opened and Abe came out. 'Thomas is right. Don't you go getting yourselves into trouble cos of me. Hand me in. But before you do, tell me this, what did you see? What happened to this *other soldier*?'

'He got beaten up,' said Lily. 'By his own officers. For being with a local girl.'

Abe's face tightened. 'Was he black?'

Lily nodded.

Abe swallowed. 'Figures.'

'I don't get it. What does it matter if a soldier's black and takes a lady to get chips?' Pattie burst out.

'It shouldn't matter but it does,' said Abe bitterly. 'Because that's the way it is in the American Army.' He tugged his army jacket. 'If you're black and low-ranking like me, they think it gives them licence to abuse you. It's why I ran.' He shook his head. 'We've come here to help, but our own officers treat us like dirt. Why, when we arrived, they even went round the eating places asking the owners to *do what they do back at home* – put signs in the windows saying no black folks allowed so the whites can drink alone.'

'That's awful,' said Pattie, looking as shocked as Lily felt.

'But some people in the village said no,' Abe went on. 'They told the officers we don't do that here and they put up signs *welcoming* us.' His jaw clenched. 'That just riled the officers even more and the other night they came into a pub where a bunch of us were drinking. They started a fight, shouting about how they'd got it

157

right back home with the lynchings and beating of black people and with black people being kept out of white folks' way.' He shook his head, his face clouded with the memory.

Lily couldn't believe it. How could people treat other people like that?

'Some of the black soldiers fought back,' said Abe. 'More officers arrived and they started handcuffing people. But it was only soldiers that look like me that were arrested. They even shot one guy. I . . . well, I panicked.' He looked at the ground. 'I went out the back door of the pub and vaulted over a wall but I fell and that's how I hurt my leg and ankle. I got away, though, and I didn't stop moving till I found your hideout.'

'I'm glad you did find it,' said Thomas.

Abe gave him a grateful look. 'So, as you can see, it's not all it seems. Sure, I'm a deserter but can you see now why I couldn't stay?'

They nodded.

'If they catch me, they'll lock me up or . . . or worse.' Abe's voice faltered.

'Worse?' echoed Thomas.

'What's worse than prison?' said Pattie.

'Hanging,' said Abe flatly.

Both Pattie and Ted moved closer to Lily, looking up at her as if hoping she would tell them that this wasn't real, that Abe was just kidding. She put her arms round them, wishing she could reassure them but knowing Abe was telling the truth. Anger rose up inside her. This was so wrong!

'But . . . you're a soldier,' said Thomas, looking like he was trying to make sense of it. 'They wouldn't hang you, would they?'

'They can do whatever they please,' said Abe heavily. 'They already have – to others.'

Lily wanted to be sick.

'So I'm begging you,' Abe went on desperately. 'Please don't hand me in. Just let me escape. I'll go tonight, under cover of darkness. If I can find a way to Liverpool, I'll get myself on to a boat and sail home.'

Lily looked at Thomas. She knew what she wanted but it was his bedroom, his house . . .

'Don't go,' he said. 'Stay here until your leg's better. We won't tell anyone.'

Lily felt like throwing her arms round him. She beamed at him and he blushed.

Abe looked like he was about to argue.

'No,' she said, stopping him as he opened his mouth. 'It's sorted. We're going to help you escape!'

CHAPTER EIGHTEEN

On the way downstairs Thomas overheard a low conversation between his gran, his mum and Great-Uncle Walter in the hall. Thomas couldn't hear everything they were saying but the worry in their voices was plain and he heard Gran saying they had to stay positive. *About what?* thought Thomas, anxiety spiralling through him. Could they have heard something about his dad? No, if there was bad news, surely they would have told him?

He pushed his worries down. They were probably just talking about the war generally and right now he had other things to worry about. If Abe was found in his bedroom, they were all going to be in so much trouble and Abe . . . well, Thomas didn't want to think what would happen to him. *He's a boy*, Thomas thought, the

161

unfairness of it beating through him. *Not a man. He shouldn't be here. He should be back home with his mum. It's wrong if they punish him for leaving.*

That night Bobbie and Annie put out the blue-and-white crockery and silver cutlery that they kept for special occasions. They had used their meat rations to buy enough beef to serve up a delicious stew with dumplings and fresh carrots and peas from the garden followed by rhubarb and custard. Uncle Walter kept everyone entertained, talking, telling jokes and even pretending to be the prime minister Winston Churchill at one point. Thomas usually loved Uncle Walter's performances but he was too worried to relax.

The others seemed to enjoy it, though. Afterwards Lily asked Uncle Walter what his job was. 'Are you important?' she asked.

Uncle Walter chuckled. 'Me? Let's just say I'm a small cog in a vast machine. I work in a large department making sure our war effort is as efficient as it might be. I speak with other countries – our allies – and make sure we all know what each other is thinking . . .'

'Do you ever speak with the Americans?' Pattie interrupted him eagerly.

'Sometimes.' Uncle Walter looked curious. 'Why?'

'No reason,' Thomas cut in, scared Pattie was going to give the game away.

Uncle Walter frowned slightly. 'Thomas, it was Pattie who asked the question.'

'Yes, but . . .'

'Let her talk,' said Uncle Walter, looking at Pattie. Thomas felt his heart speeding up. What would Pattie say?

'Are Americans our friends – in the war?' she said.

Uncle Walter smiled at her. 'Very much so. It took them a while to join but, now that they have, they're fighting with us, side by side.'

Pattie looked puzzled and like she was about to say something else but then to Thomas's relief, she appeared to think better of it and subsided into silence.

After they'd all helped clear away, Bobbie shooed them off to bed. Thomas lay awake in the dark listening to the sound of Abe breathing in the games cupboard, his brain swirling. How were they going to get Abe on to a train to Liverpool without being found out? And what about Abe's leg? It was still bad. How long would he need to rest before he was well enough to travel?

He jumped as he heard a gentle knock on his door. 'Are you awake, young man?' It was Uncle Walter.

'Yes,' said Thomas nervously, wondering what he wanted.

'Sorry to disturb you,' said Uncle Walter, coming in. 'But your mother says the backgammon set is in your cupboard.' He smiled. 'And she and I have a score to settle. I'll just fetch it —'

'No!' Thomas leaped out of bed.

'What?' said Uncle Walter in surprise.

'It's not in there,' Thomas gabbled.

'Your mother definitely said it was —'

'I moved it!'

Uncle Walter frowned. 'So where is it?'

Just then Thomas's mum put her head round the door. 'Have you got it?'

'Thomas says he moved it,' said Uncle Walter.

'Nonsense. It was there yesterday,' she said, marching to the cupboard.

'Mum! It's not in there any more!' Thomas said, panicked. 'It's —'

He was too late. His mum whipped the cupboard open. Thomas cringed, waiting for an exclamation of shock but it never came. His mum grabbed the backgammon set and, as she turned, Thomas saw that Abe had hidden himself under a blanket beneath the bottom shelf. Annie shut the cupboard door. 'Backgammon!' she said triumphantly to Uncle Walter. 'The game is on!'

Uncle Walter followed her out, chuckling.

Thomas was overwhelmed by a tidal wave of relief. He flopped down on his bed, his heart gradually slowing and then he opened the cupboard again.

Abe was still concealed.

'Abe, it's just me,' Thomas whispered.

Abe's head poked out from under the blanket. 'Hell, that was close.'

'You'll have to get out of here tomorrow,' said Thomas

urgently. 'I wish you could stay for longer until your leg is healed but it's just not safe.'

Abe nodded. 'I'll go soon as the coast is clear.'

The next morning, Thomas was keen to leave for school so that he could talk to Lily about Abe and about getting him out of his bedroom. Just as they were going to leave, his mum came hurrying to find them. She was holding an envelope.

'The mail's arrived and there's a letter for you three,' she said. 'It looks like it's from home.' She turned it round so they could see a big heart drawn on the back.

'It's from our mum!' said Lily.

'Read it! Read it!' Ted said in excitement.

'You can read it on the way to school,' said Annie, handing Lily the letter. 'Just don't be late.'

'Let's stop in the graveyard and read it there,' Lily said as they headed out into the sunny morning. The air smelled fresh and delicate spider webs stretched among the flowers, the dew drops on them glittering like tiny diamonds. Lily grabbed Ted's hand and started to run with Pattie close behind then. Thomas followed more slowly. He was glad they had a letter but it made him think of his dad. It really had been ages now since they'd had a letter from him. Thinking of the whispered conversation he'd heard and his mum's strange behaviour, he felt the same sharp worry niggle at him again. Maybe there *was* something the grown-ups weren't telling him about his dad. *I need to ask Mum about it*, he decided. *As soon as we've sorted out what to do with Abe, I'll speak to her.*

Lily climbed over the wall into the graveyard. She didn't go near to where the bomb had fallen but stopped close to the house and sat on one of the graves that looked like a giant table. Opening the envelope, she spread the letter out on the grey stone. *'Dear Lily and Ted –'* Pattie looked expectant – *'and your new friend, Thomas,'* Lily said, her eyes twinkling. *'All good here . . .'*

'What?' Pattie exclaimed, outraged. 'It doesn't say that, Lily! It doesn't!'

She tried to grab the letter but Lily held it out of her reach. 'Looks like she must have forgotten about you,' she teased.

'Give it me, Lily! Give it!' Pattie cried. Jumping up, she managed to grab it. Reading the first line she gave her sister a triumphant look. '*Dear* Pattie, *Lily and Ted, all good here and please don't worry. We are safe and life goes on as normal as we can make it. It was amazing to receive your letter – I read it five times. All the girls at the hospital thought I was mad because I kept reading parts aloud to them. It was so nice to hear—*'

Lily gasped. 'That's it!'

'Don't interrupt,' Pattie told her crossly.

'No, *listen*!' said Lily. 'I know what to do about Abe now.'

They all stared.

'What do you mean?' said Thomas.

'Our mum's a nurse. If we can get Abe to her, she can help treat his leg and then, when he's better, she can help him get home.'

Thomas looked at her as if she was mad. 'And how are we going to get him to your mum? She's in *Manchester*!'

Lily grinned. 'Yes, and the train stops there on the way to Liverpool!'

Thomas frowned. 'So, you won't let me tell my mum but you're happy to tell your mum?' That didn't seem fair to him.

'It's different,' Lily said.

'Why?' He didn't see any difference at all.

'My mum's not a headmistress,' Lily pointed out. 'And Abe hasn't gone missing in *her* village.'

'That doesn't matter,' Thomas protested. 'I know my mum will help Abe if we tell her about him.'

Lily shook her head. 'No, Thomas, she won't.'

'She—'

'You don't get it!' Lily interrupted sharply. 'I know you want to help but you don't understand. You're not like us. We *know* about war, about how awful it is.'

'And I don't?' exclaimed Thomas hotly.

'No. You don't,' Lily said. 'Not properly, because you haven't lost anyone.'

Thomas was confused. What was she going on about? Her mum was alive and her dad was fighting just like his. 'Who have you lost then?'

'Our dad,' said Pattie, her lower lip trembling. 'He was killed.'

Thomas didn't understand. What did Pattie mean? Their dad wasn't dead. Lily had told him. 'But you said he was away fighting—'

'I lied, okay?' Lily cut across him. 'He died in combat last year.'

Ted gave a sudden sob and Lily put her arm round him.

Thomas didn't know what to say. He was reeling from the revelation. 'I'm . . . I'm sorry,' he stammered. And he really was. He felt incredibly sorry for them but he also felt a growing anger. Lily had lied to him. They all had. He'd thought they were his friends but they hadn't told him the truth. Their betrayal stung – Lily's most of all. 'Why didn't you tell me?' he said. 'Why did you lie?'

Lily sighed. 'I'm sorry. We'd only just met when you asked about him. I hardly knew you and didn't want to talk about it. Every time we do, one of us cries.'

Thomas swallowed. He guessed he could understand

it, but knowing they'd been keeping such a massive thing secret changed something for him. Instead of it being all of them all together, it now felt like they were separate from him.

I don't want to do this any more. The thought suddenly hit him. *I don't want the lies, the secrets, the hiding things . . .*

He backed away. 'You'll never get Abe to your mum, Lily. It's impossible.'

'Well, we'll go back to the original plan and get him straight to Liverpool then,' said Lily. 'We'll find as much medicine and bandages as we can and help him get the train to the dock where he can get on a boat and—'

'No,' Thomas interrupted. 'Lily, stop this now! We're going to do the right thing. We're telling the grown-ups the truth and then whatever happens, happens.'

'Tom!' she exclaimed. He started at her using the short form of his name – only his mum usually did that. 'For heaven's sake! You're a great lad, you really are, but you just don't get that sometimes you need to keep secrets and sort things out for yourself and not tell the grown-ups.' She let out a frustrated exclamation. 'You don't know how things work – you don't know how *life* works!'

'Meaning?' Thomas demanded.

'Meaning that all you've ever known is happiness! That's brilliant but it's not like that for people like *us*. In the city you need to be smart, take risks, tell untruths, keep secrets. You have to! It's called survival.'

Thomas felt a hot rush of anger. He was fed up of her telling him he didn't understand – that he didn't get it. 'No, Lily!' he said hotly. 'It's called being a *liar*. And that might suit you but not me. I'm not going to be a liar. Not now, not ever.'

They glared at each other.

Thomas's thoughts raced. What should he do now? He badly wanted to tell his mum but deep in his heart he knew Lily was right. His mum was the headmistress in the village; she would feel it was her duty to tell the military police and hand Abe in. And then what would happen to Abe?

Thomas made up his mind. 'Fine. You've got today,'

he said flatly. 'But just today. You work out a plan to get Abe on the train or I'm telling them he's here.'

Lily's face relaxed with relief. With a smile, she stepped towards him but he didn't feel like making up. With a shake of his head, he turned and marched away, blinking back the tears that stung his eyes.

CHAPTER NINETEEN

Lily felt awful. She knew she'd hurt Thomas by lying about their dad. *It wasn't my fault*, she thought defensively. *Why would I tell someone I'd just met about something like that? And it would have upset Ted and Pattie . . .*

But despite what she told herself, deep down she knew she was in the wrong. Even if she had lied to Thomas at first, she should have told him the truth when they became friends. *I'll make it up to him*, she thought with a sigh. *But first I need to help Abe escape.*

She wasn't sure if Thomas would carry through his threat of telling his mum but she couldn't risk it. She knew Abe hadn't been making it up when he'd said the army might hang him for deserting. War made people – even people fighting on the side of good – do awful, dreadful things.

By lunchtime she'd come up with a plan. She pulled Pattie over to a quiet corner of the playground. 'I'm going to sneak on to the Liverpool train after school with Abe and I'm going to help him get there safely and on a boat.'

'I'm coming with you,' Pattie said immediately.

'No,' said Lily firmly. There was no way she was risking Pattie being arrested for helping a deserter.

'Lily, if you're going away, then I want to come with you!'

'You can't. If you come, then we'll have to take Ted and he's too little. Also, the more of us that go, the more chance there is of us getting caught. I'll be back soon.'

'I'm coming,' insisted Pattie.

'You're not!'

'I am!'

'Not!'

'Am!'

'Not!'

'Am!' Pattie flicked Lily's nose with her fingers.

'Ow!' Lily spread her hands. 'Okay, fine,' she said as if she'd given in. 'You can tell Ted, though. Go on, go and tell him we're leaving him here.'

Pattie hesitated and looked across the playground to where Ted was playing football with some of the other younger boys. Lily saw her shoulders sink and nodded to herself. She'd known Pattie wouldn't be able to do it.

'You're horrible.' Pattie kicked her crossly and stomped away.

Lily rubbed her ankle, grimacing, but at least part one of her plan was complete – Pattie and Ted were going to stay here where they'd be safe. Now she needed to get Abe and start part two of her plan – the escape!

After school, Lily raced home ahead of the others. Thomas had barely spoken to her all day. He seemed to have forgiven Ted and Pattie, though, and was chatting as usual with them as the three of them walked back along the high street.

Lily was relieved to find the house empty. She grabbed a few things from the kitchen and then ran up the stairs and pulled open the cupboard in Thomas's room. Abe leaped to his feet in alarm, his face relaxing when he saw it was only her.

'Time to go!' she said. 'It's now or never. There's a train in an hour.'

'Okay. But no making me wear lady's clothes this time. Deal?'

Lily grinned. 'Deal. I'll get you some clothes that belong to Thomas's dad. You can't go in your uniform.'

She fetched him some clothes and waited while he got changed, then they left. Abe hobbled – his leg was clearly still really hurting him. Lily watched anxiously as he used the banister to take his weight as he made his way down the stairs. He winced with every step. Once they were downstairs, she offered him her arm to lean on but he shook his head.

'Fine,' she said, rolling her eyes, 'but come on – we've got to hurry!'

They cut through the graveyard, sticking to the paths, which were easier for Abe to hobble on. Lily could feel the worry building inside her. The longer they were outside, the more chance there was that someone was going to see them. As they reached the field with the chickens in, Lily's eyes fell on the old tractor near to the coop and an idea popped into her head.

'Abe,' she said, pointing at the tractor.

He followed her gaze and realised what she was thinking. 'You've gotta be joking!'

'You want to get on that train, don't you? It'll be a lot faster and after all . . .' Lily ran over and climbed into the passenger's seat. 'You're a soldier,' she said. 'You've got to know how to drive, right?'

They looked at each other and the look turned into smiles. Lily felt excitement sweep through her. This was turning into a proper adventure!

Abe turned the handle at the front of the tractor and the engine fired up. Leaning out, Lily offered Abe her hand. He took it and struggled up into the seat beside her then he pressed the accelerator and they set off, trundling across the first field and into the next, Lily helped by reaching over to work the brakes and by jumping down to open the gates. As they came through one, they saw an old lady walking her dog. Lily recognised her as Mrs Wilkes from the post office.

'Quick! Go! Go! Go!' she hissed to Abe. She knew Mrs Wilkes was very nosy.

'This is the fastest it goes – it's a tractor!' Abe exclaimed.

They chugged past. Mrs Wilkes looked surprised. Lily knew there was only one thing to do – brazen it out and act like there was absolutely nothing strange about them driving a tractor across the field. She nodded at Mrs Wilkes and carried on towards the station.

Glancing back, she could see the puzzled frown on Mrs Wilkes's face. She called her dog and then turned and hurried back in the direction of the village. Lily groaned inwardly. She had a feeling Mrs Wilkes was going to tell people. All she could hope was that she and Abe could get on to the Liverpool train before anyone realised what was going on and tried to stop them.

They parked the tractor by the junkyard. The train was just pulling into the station, belching out smoke like a huge dragon. Lily helped Abe over the wall and they ran through the junkyard towards the platform.

'How are you doing?' Lily asked.

'I'm okay,' said Abe but she could see his face was rigid with pain as he hobbled. 'Is that the train?'

'Yes, yes, it is!' said Lily, pulling him by the hand. She'd memorised the timetable. 'Come on!'

They were nearly at the platform when Thomas stepped out from behind an old carriage. 'What are you doing here?' Lily demanded.

'Pattie said you were going to the railway so I guessed you had something mad planned,' he said.

'Abe's getting on the Liverpool train,' said Lily. She took a breath. 'And I'm going with him. I'll help him find a ship to get on, then come back. Can you look after Pattie and Ted while I'm gone?'

'Of course,' Thomas said, to her relief. 'But I'm telling you you'll never make it on to that train –' he paused and then smiled – 'without my help.'

Lily stared at him. 'What do you mean?'

'You need a distraction so you can get on without being seen.' Thomas squared his shoulders. 'Well, that's where I come in!'

❋   ❋   ❋

People were boarding the train, Richard helping them with their luggage. The station master was standing near the waiting room, watching what was going on. The doors started to shut and the guard blew his whistle.

Thomas popped his head out from behind a trolley piled high with crates and baskets and boxes. Chickens clucked in several of the crates. Lily saw Thomas draw his arm back and then with a very accurate aim he launched an egg into the air. It hit the elderly station master on the back. He shouted in alarm and swung round angrily. 'Oi! Who threw that?'

Thomas chucked another one. It fell on the platform, splattering everywhere.

'Come 'ere, you young scoundrel!' shouted the station master. He set off towards Thomas, who darted back towards the junkyard. The station master gave chase. 'I'll 'ave your guts for garters!'

'This is our chance!' Lily hissed to Abe. She grabbed Abe's arm and they made a run for it. Fear of being caught temporarily masked Abe's pain and he reached one of the end carriages just as the train was starting to puff and pull away. Turning the handle, he pulled the door open and clambered on board.

Lily was still running alongside the train. 'Help me!'

'You sure about this?' cried Abe.

Lily nodded and he reached out his hand. She caught it and he hauled her on to the train beside him, slamming the door shut after her. For a moment she leaned against the walls, gasping for breath, hardly able to believe they'd done it – they'd got on to the train. She staggered to the open window. The station was speeding past but as they passed the door that led to the platform from the ticket office, she saw Thomas had doubled back and was running along, waving goodbye. She waved back and then saw something that made her heart somersault – a police officer running on to the platform, his face falling as he saw the train speeding away.

'We did it!' said Abe. 'We got away.'

Watching as the police officer thumped his hand down on Thomas's shoulder and swung him round, Lily hoped he was right.

CHAPTER TWENTY

Abe and Lily crouched together in the small toilet cubicle as the train swayed from side to side, steaming along the track. They had decided to hide in there to avoid the guard. They were sharing the provisions Lily had grabbed from the kitchen before they'd left – a couple of apples and a small bar of chocolate.

'Liverpool, here we come!' she said.

But as she spoke there was a squealing hissing sound and the train slowed down. It jolted to a halt, throwing Lily and Abe against the toilet walls.

'Why have we stopped?' said Abe in alarm.

Lily got to her feet, craning to see out of the top of the frosted-glass window in the toilet. 'I don't know. I can't see anything from in here.' She felt worried. 'I'll go and see what's going on. Lock the door when I leave.'

Lily let herself out of the toilet and walked along the side corridor that ran alongside the compartments. In each compartment she could see people turning to each other and standing up to peer out of the window. She felt very uneasy.

Just as she was about to open the door and walk into the next carriage, she saw something through the glass panel in the door that made her freeze. A group of American military police in khaki uniforms with white belts were at the far end of the corridor. They were opening the compartment doors and talking to the people inside. They were clearly searching for something – or someone.

Lily recognised one of them as the sergeant who had hit the soldier outside the chippy and she knew without the shadow of a doubt that they were looking for Abe – they had to be!

Swearing under her breath, she turned and doubled back, sprinting to the toilet cubicle. 'Abe! It's me!' she hissed, thumping the door.

He opened it and she crashed inside. 'Quick! We have to find somewhere better to hide!'

'Why? What is it?' he said in alarm.

'Army. Loads of them! I bet they're searching for us . . . come on!'

They left the cubicle and hurried along the train, away from the military police officers. Lily scanned every nook and cranny. Where could they hide? The compartments were no good. There were just the benches and luggage nets but as they reached the next carriage, her heart lifted. It was a large carriage for goods and luggage! There were crates with pigeons and chickens inside and boxes, suitcases and trunks all piled high. 'We can hide in here!'

Abe hobbled to the end of the carriage and climbed into a large wicker basket.

Lily found a hiding space on a shelf. Pulling a rug over herself, she held her breath, her heart pounding as she heard the stomp of boots and the shouts of the officers getting louder and louder.

Please don't find us, she prayed. *Please just go away.*

The carriage door was shoved open. From her hiding place she could just see out. A pair of boots stomped towards her and she heard a cigarette lighter being flicked on and off as the officer walked through the carriage. She hardly dared to breathe. Her heart was beating so loudly, she was sure he'd be able to hear it.

Flick. Flick. The officer struck the lighter on and off with each slow step. He reached the end of the carriage and swung round. 'All clear in here!' he shouted.

Lily sagged with relief as he started to march back towards the door but suddenly his footsteps stopped. There was a pause that made her hair prickle. What was going on?

She held her breath and then, to her dismay, she heard him walking quickly over to where Abe was hiding.

The next second, he was blowing his whistle loudly. 'They're here! I've found one of them!' he bellowed.

Everything seemed to happen at once. Lily heard Abe yell and she jumped to her feet. There was the pounding of feet and shouting as officers piled into the carriage and then Lily felt her arms being grabbed by a pair of strong hands.

'Get off me!' she said furiously. She kicked out and heard the officer holding her swear but he didn't let go. Across the room, she could see Abe trying to fight two officers off, but it was no use. They were bigger and stronger than he was and within minutes they had snapped handcuffs on him.

'You're coming with us, boy!' snarled one of the officers, shoving him towards the door. Abe stumbled and cried out in pain.

'No!' Lily shouted. 'You can't take him! You can't do this!' Her fury gave her strength and, wrenching herself free, she launched herself at the officer who had shoved Abe. She pummelled his chest.

He grabbed her hands, his grip like iron. 'You little vixen! You're coming too!'

Lily felt handcuffs being snapped on to her wrist.

'Into the truck with them!' the officer commanded. 'They're both under arrest!'

CHAPTER TWENTY-ONE

Meanwhile, back in Oakworth, Thomas was in the station waiting room also under arrest. He'd told the policeman that he didn't know who the girl and boy were who had just got on to the train but then the station master had come puffing back on to the platform.

'Arrest 'im, officer!' he'd cried. 'That lad threw two eggs at me. He was helping those two who hopped on to the train without a ticket.'

'Right, you're coming with me,' the policeman said to him.

He'd taken Thomas to the waiting room. Thomas had been in there for what felt like hours. The policeman had sent the station boy with a message to Annie but before she arrived a Jeep full of military police officers had turned up.

'What do you know about Abraham McCarthy?' demanded the officer in charge, standing over Thomas, his eyes hard.

'I don't know anything,' muttered Thomas.

The officers kept questioning him but knowing how they treated soldiers like Abe, Thomas stayed silent. He wasn't going to help them. They could shout at him all they liked but he knew they couldn't hurt him.

At long last he heard his mum's voice. 'Where's my son? What's happened? I want to see him now!'

'Please come this way, Mrs Clark,' Thomas heard an officer say. 'We need to speak to you about a very serious matter . . .'

Annie burst into the room with Uncle Walter close behind.

'Stand,' the military officer said to Thomas.

But he was already on his feet, tears springing to his eyes. 'Mum . . .'

She was next to him in a flash, embracing him tightly. He could feel her fury as she glared at the officers. 'What is going on here?' she said in a voice that could have cut through steel. 'I demand an explanation!'

In next to no time Thomas was released. As his mum pointed out, the police had no grounds for holding him there. There was no proof he knew anything about Abe and Lily. Uncle Walter drove them home. On the way they told Thomas that Abe and Lily had been captured on the train and taken away.

'You've got to help them!' Thomas pleaded.

'I'll do what I can to find out where they've been taken,' said Uncle Walter sombrely.

Thomas's mum put a hand to her forehead. 'What am I going to say to Lily's mother? If we can even get hold of her.'

'I'll go and make some phone calls,' said Uncle Walter.

Leaving them outside the house, he headed back to the village centre.

Thomas's mum shook her head as she watched him

go and then turned to Thomas. 'You should have told me what was going on. I thought we told each other everything.'

Thomas gazed at her. 'But do we?'

There was a long pause and he saw a look of fear flit across her face. He swallowed. He couldn't wait any longer. He had to know if she was hiding something. 'Are you telling me everything – about Daddy?'

His mum hesitated, seeming like she was trying to work out what to say.

'Mum. Please,' he said. He felt like someone was twisting his stomach. 'Is he dead?'

'No, he isn't,' his mum said quickly. Thomas felt a surge of relief. 'And you're right. I should have told you what was going on, but I was protecting you – well, trying to. I didn't know exactly what was going on and I didn't want you to worry.'

'Like Gran does with you,' said Thomas.

'Yes, like Gran does with me,' agreed his mum.

'And you hate it,' he reminded her.

She nodded. 'I'm sorry, Tom, but I've been worried

sick and because I didn't have all the information I thought it best not to say anything . . .'

'What do you mean?' he demanded. 'What's happened to him? Tell me!'

His mum reached out and took his hand. He could see from her face that this was hard for her but he had to know. 'Your dad's plane got shot down. He parachuted and survived but he was captured.' She swallowed. 'He's in a camp for prisoners of war but we've just heard today that he's all right. There are others in there with him and Uncle Walter can keep track of him now.'

Thomas faltered. 'Will they . . . hurt him?'

'No, they won't,' his mum said, but he could see from her face it was a hope not a certainty. She lifted her chin and spoke more strongly. 'And when all this nonsense is over we'll get him back. We have German soldiers here in England. We'll give them back and the Germans will give back your dad and the others he's with. The important thing is your dad's alive. He's alive and we have to cling to that.'

'I hate war!' said Thomas, trying not to cry as he

thought of his dad in a prisoner-of-war camp. 'I *hate* it! Lily's dad died. And Abe's brother. And for what? The whole thing is stupid!'

'Thomas,' his mum said, reaching to hug him but he pulled away. A hug couldn't solve what was going on.

'No! I just want Dad home and the war to be over!' He stormed off into the garden.

'Tom . . . Thomas!' his mum called but he didn't stop.

'Leave me alone!' he shouted, anger seething through him. Not at her but at the world and all the grown-ups who'd decided that everyone should fight and kill.

'Thomas!' his mum said again.

Jumping the garden wall, he headed into the graveyard without looking back.

Thomas sat on one of the undamaged tabletop graves and cried and cried. His tears had just dried when he heard footsteps on the grass and looked up to see Uncle Walter coming towards him.

He put a hand gently on Thomas's shoulder. 'It's not an easy time,' he said quietly.

Thomas sniffed. 'This morning Lily said that my life has always been good, always been happy and she's right. I've had all the horrible things kept away from me – until now.'

Uncle Walter nodded. 'Yes, and that's your family's gift to you because childhood should be special. Worry-free.'

'But the truth is the world's a bad place,' said Thomas bitterly.

'It's not, Thomas; it really isn't,' said Uncle Walter. 'Right now, yes, we're dealing with evil and it's our bad luck to have to live through that, but look at all the people trying to stop it – good people – risking their lives. Men like your father. There's a saying that all it takes for evil to flourish is for good people to do nothing. But as long as we do something, good will win – in the end.'

Thomas looked into Uncle Walter's wise face. He desperately wanted to believe him. 'How do you know?' he asked in a small voice.

'We're getting the upper hand now,' Uncle Walter said. 'With some help from our American friends.'

'But why are the officers so horrible to Abe?' said

CHAPTER TWENTY-ONE

Thomas. 'He's not the enemy – he's not a Nazi. Why are they hunting him down?'

Uncle Walter sighed. 'The US Army needs to keep discipline, even if that seems harsh at times.'

'But he's too young!' Thomas protested. 'He shouldn't even be here.'

'But he is. He chose to sign up,' said Uncle Walter patiently. 'He's an American and it's up to his superiors now to decide what happens to him. I'm not sure there's much we can do.' He rubbed his chin. 'Listen, I probably shouldn't be telling you this, but I've learned there's an American transport train coming through here tomorrow from the military base with certain *young* prisoners on board as well as senior officials. One in particular, a general, has a lot of power. I believe that if anyone can help Abe, it's him.'

'Really?' said Thomas, feeling a flicker of hope. 'When's the train coming?'

'I don't know,' said Uncle Walter. He gave Thomas a sideways look. 'But I think we both know a man who might . . .'

'Richard?' said Thomas. 'With his radio receiver!'

Uncle Walter nodded.

The flicker of hope inside Thomas turned into a flame. Maybe there *was* something they could do after all! But he couldn't do it on his own; he'd need some help – lots of help. But how could he get that?

An answer popped into his head and he jumped off the grave. He didn't know if it would work, but he had to try!

CHAPTER TWENTY-TWO

Lily hugged her knees to her chest. It was cold in the army base and all she had was a single rough blanket to keep her warm. The military police had taken her and Abe to a room that had been split into compartments separated by wire mesh. They'd said it was just for the night and the next day they were going to be put on a train. After that, she had no idea what was going to happen.

Lily pulled the blanket round her more tightly and shuffled closer to the mesh panel that separated her and Abe. He had been sleeping sitting up, resting against the wall, but now he looked at her. 'You okay?'

Lily nodded, although she didn't feel okay. She felt scared and lost, worried about what Pattie and Ted would

197

be thinking, but most of all worried about what was going to happen to Abe.

'You ever been in trouble before?' Abe asked her.

'Yeah. Loads,' said Lily, trying to act like it was no big deal.

It didn't fool Abe. 'But not like this, right?'

Lily bit her lip and then shook her head. 'No, not like this,' she admitted, fighting back the tears that were threatening to creep from her eyes.

Back at home, Thomas ran into the kitchen. He was feeling much better now he'd thought of a plan and there was something he could do rather than just sitting around. Pattie and Ted were at the table with untouched jacket potatoes in front of them. Pattie had her arms round Ted, who was in tears.

'Have you heard anything more?' she asked Thomas. 'Where's our Lily? When are the army going to let her go?'

'I don't know,' said Thomas. 'Soon, though, I hope.'

'What about Abe?' Pattie went on. 'Will the Americans do what he said they would?'

'No!' Ted burst out, his sobs increasing.

'I hope not. I'm going to try and get them to release him,' said Thomas.

'How?' said Pattie in astonishment.

'I've got a plan,' said Thomas. 'But I'll need lots of people for it to work – all the kids from the village and all the evacuees. Do you reckon you can help me persuade the evacuees? They'll listen to you more than me.'

'I'll try,' said Pattie, looking excited. 'But what about the village kids?'

'I've got a plan for that!' said Thomas. 'Come on! Let's go!'

'You want *me* to help *you*?' Georgie stood on his doorstep, staring at Thomas as if he'd grown three heads. 'Why would I do that?'

'Because what's happening to Abe isn't fair,' Thomas said quickly. 'He's only fourteen – a year older than us and they're going to put him in prison or worse. All he was trying to do was to get home to his mum. It's not right. They shouldn't punish him for that.'

Georgie hesitated but then shook his head. 'No, they shouldn't,' he said. 'Bloomin' grown-ups.'

'You can help, Georgie,' Thomas said. 'If anyone can get the other kids to join in, it's you.'

Georgie looked pleased. 'You think?'

'I know!' said Thomas.

'All right then!' Georgie declared. 'What do I do?'

Thomas quickly told Georgie his plan. 'The American train's coming through here tomorrow after lunch. We've got to make it stop so I can talk to the general who's on it. We're going to make some giant banners with messages on and hold them up so he sees them and stops the train.'

'Sounds like a daft idea to me,' said Georgie. He shrugged. 'But better than just standing around.'

Thomas smiled as he remembered Lily's words. 'Like lemons,' he said.

'You what?' said Georgie, mystified.

Thomas shook his head, hoping that Lily was okay wherever she was. 'It doesn't matter. Just meet tomorrow morning by the graveyard at eight, okay?'

'What about school?' said Georgie.

CHAPTER TWENTY-TWO

Thomas lifted his chin. 'We'll have to skip it. This is much more important.'

'Now you're talking!' said Georgie with a grin. 'I'll be seeing you at eight then.' He spat on his hand and held it out. Thomas hesitated and then grinned, spat on his own hand and they shook.

Thomas walked away up the street, his heart singing. His plan was in motion. Now he just had to hope it worked!

The next morning, Thomas, Pattie and Ted got up as the sun was starting to rise over the hills. They took some old sheets from the linen chest and fetched paint and brushes from the garden, then they met Georgie and set off round the village, knocking on doors, asking everyone to help. The choice between going to school or joining in with something fun was not a hard one and most of the children from school willingly agreed to join in. Those who didn't received a narrow-eyed stare from Georgie and quickly changed their minds.

Soon everyone was gathered in Thomas's garden, the

air alive with a feeling of excitement and anticipation. Pattie and Ted handed out brushes and paints and Thomas issued instructions as to what to write.

Looking up at the window, he saw his mum, gran and Uncle Walter watching. He could tell they were wondering what on earth was going on but to his relief his mum just gave him a nod and a smile and didn't try to stop them. His gran looked positively delighted to see the crowd of children all working together and headed down to the kitchen to make a huge batch of rock cakes that she handed around while the paint on the banners dried.

'Now this is what I like to see!' she declared, her eyes shining. 'Action!'

When the rock cakes had been devoured, Thomas, Georgie, Pattie and Ted led the way across the fields with a snake of chattering children behind them. Thinking about it the night before, Thomas had decided that the best place to hold up the banners was where the railway track came near to the river.

The clear water of the river bubbled and splashed over

the rocks. The children crossed the expanse of water by slipping and sliding on a path of stepping stones and then they all scrambled up the steep scrubby bank to where the railway track was. Thomas unfolded the three banners and directed people where to stand. One group took the first banner, which read LOOK OUT IN FRONT!, and another group took the second banner, which read PLEASE STOP!, and the third took the banner that said PLEASE STOP! THIS IS AN EMERGENCY.

'The train's coming!' cried Pattie, pointing along the track to where a dark grey military train could be seen in the distance. Puffs of white steam poured out of its central funnel as it chugged along the tracks.

Thomas yelled. 'Now!'

The children lifted the banners and anyone not holding a banner waved their arms wildly. The train drew closer and closer.

Please work, thought Thomas. *Please stop!*

The train slowed and for one wonderful moment Thomas thought his plan had worked, but then it started to build up speed again. He felt a rush of despair. He wished Lily was there. What would she do?

Suddenly he knew! He sprinted down the bank towards the track, jumped over the rails and sleepers and stopped in the middle of the tracks, waving wildly.

The enormous train steamed towards him. The sound of the engine grew louder in his ears, a mountain of sound blocking out everything else. *The driver hasn't seen me,* Thomas thought, feeling completely terrified but knowing he couldn't give up.

'Stop! Please stop!' he yelled.

CHAPTER TWENTY-THREE

Thomas heard the wonderful sound of the wheels turning slower and slower and steam hissing as the train came to a stop, the great black engine only a short distance from where he was standing. Thomas's legs were shaking so badly he could hardly stand. Glancing to the side he saw the other children whooping and Pattie and Ted hugging each other in relief. He'd stopped the train!

But that was only the start of his plan, he remembered, as a door opened and a group of smartly dressed officials stepped out on to the track, led by a very distinguished-looking black general.

'Thomas!' Pattie shouted, running down the bank with the other children. She reached him first and flung her arms round him. 'I'm so glad you're safe!'

The officers approached him, angry looks on their faces.

The children all gathered closer to Thomas as if to share the brunt of the grown-ups' anger.

'What the hell are you doing?' demanded the general, looking at Thomas.

Thomas longed to run away but he fixed his mind on Abe and Lily and met the general's angry gaze. 'Sorry to stop your train, sir,' he said, noticing that Uncle Walter's car had just drawn up on the dirt track that ran alongside the top of the bank and that his mum, gran and Uncle Walter were all jumping out. 'But we want to join the army.'

The officials looked at each other, their faces relaxing slightly.

'Yeah,' said Pattie, stepping forward, clutching Ted's hand. 'We want to sign up – all of us. We want to fight in the war.'

The officers' smiles broadened and a few of them even chuckled.

The general laughed. 'Well, I applaud your spirit and

your commitment to your country, kids, but I'm afraid you're all a little young.'

'But we want to,' said Ted seriously.

Thomas nodded. 'Yes, we do. Don't we?' he said, looking around.

There was a chorus of replies.

'Yeah.'

'Please let us join.'

'We want to be in the army and fight!'

The general looked like he didn't quite know what to make of all the shouting children. 'Well, that's admirable but I'm afraid you need to stay in school and let our brave soldiers do the fighting.'

'So what you're saying is we can't be soldiers at eleven or twelve?' Thomas said, pointing at various kids. 'At thirteen or fourteen?'

'I'm afraid not, son,' said the general, shaking his head.

'Why?' asked Thomas, seeing that Mum, Gran and Uncle Walter had stopped nearby and were taking the conversation in.

'Because you are children and you need to be here, safe at home,' the general told him.

'Well said, sir,' Gran called loudly. '*Children* need to be safe at home. I couldn't agree more.'

The general noticed the three adults for the first time as they joined the group of children beside the tracks. 'Ma'am, what is this? What's all this about?' he said, starting to frown.

'I believe our friends are on your train,' said Thomas. 'Abraham McCarthy and Lily Watts.'

'That's my sister!' said Ted.

One of the military police officers stepped forward. 'Sir, the girl is in serious trouble for aiding and abetting Private McCarthy, a US Army deserter.'

'A deserter who's fourteen years old,' Thomas pointed out, looking directly at the general.

'That's not correct, sir,' said the officer.

'It is! It is the truth!' exclaimed Pattie.

The general looked troubled. 'Get Private McCarthy out here now – and the girl.'

The officer looked like he wanted to argue but he

obeyed the order and marched back to the train. A few minutes later, he reappeared with Abe and Lily, both in handcuffs.

Ted gasped in delight, waving madly. 'Lily!'

Lily smiled but Thomas saw how pale she looked; there were dark circles under her eyes as if she hadn't slept and her hair was escaping from its plaits. Abe looked just as exhausted and was wincing with pain as he walked. The officers made them stop in front of the general.

'Private McCarthy,' the general snapped. 'How old are you?'

'I'm fourteen, sir,' Abe said wearily.

The general frowned. 'Even if that were true, am I right in thinking you joined the army out of your own volition?'

Abe nodded. 'Yes, sir. I did. I joined to fight in the war like so many others, like my brother who died for our country because the Nazis don't like folk different to themselves.' His eyes narrowed. 'Well, let's just say they're not the only ones.'

'What do you mean, soldier?' asked the general, his voice becoming more gentle.

Abe looked from side to side at the two officers flanking him. 'I think *you* know, sir.' He shook his head. 'I know I deserted and that was wrong, but I had to leave – I had to escape our own officers.'

Both officers flanking him stared straight ahead, avoiding the general's gaze.

Abe straightened his shoulders. 'I may be fourteen but I'm no boy – not when I'm a soldier fighting for my country, risking my life.' He glanced at Lily and she smiled at him.

The general turned to the officials. 'We need to see this soldier's papers.'

Abe lifted his cuffed hands and with difficulty pulled a few photos and folded pieces of paper from his breast pocket. 'These are the only papers I have.' He unfolded them and showed them to the general. 'My beautiful brother . . . God rest his soul. And this is my mom.' He managed a smile. 'I haven't spoke to her in six months. I left her a note when I left but she's gonna be going crazy.' He handed the photo to the general, who studied it for a moment. 'She gave me this coin from the year I was born – it's meant to be lucky – and this is my birth certificate. This is how I got into the army. I just changed a number on it.' He handed the piece of paper to the general.

Annie went over curiously. 'May I see that, please, sir?'

The general looked taken aback but handed it over. Annie studied it and raised her eyebrows. 'I'm sorry, sir, but that wouldn't pass any forgery classes. The birth date has clearly been changed. Just look at it! An infant in my school could do better.'

She handed it to Uncle Walter, who laughed in astonishment. 'Dear God, who let this through? They're the ones who should be in handcuffs, not these two children.'

The general regarded Lily and Abe. 'And how about you, young lady?' he said to Lily. 'What's your story? How have you ended up involved in all this?'

Lily took a breath and met his gaze. 'My dad died for

his country just like Abe's brother and I don't think it's fair that Abe has to be punished. Why should he be just because he was prepared to risk his life so that the rest of us could have better lives? It's not right. It's an injustice, sir.'

The general nodded slowly.

'Sir . . .' Gran spoke. 'I suggest that history should be the judge of these two, not the American Army.'

Uncle Walter nodded and handed the birth certificate back to him. The general studied it for a long moment and then looked back at Abe. 'It was very courageous of you to sign up, but a child should have the right to change their mind.' He motioned to the two officers standing beside Lily and Abe. 'Let them go. Remove the handcuffs.'

'You can't do that, sir,' one of the officers protested. Thomas was sure it was the one he'd seen outside the chip shop.

The general fixed him with a steely gaze. 'Oh, indeed I can.'

'But, sir . . .'

CHAPTER TWENTY-THREE

'Do you want to wear these handcuffs, officer?' snapped the general.

Looking humiliated, the officer removed the handcuffs from Lily and Abe, who smiled at each other, looking as if they were hardly able to believe it.

'They're free!' Thomas exclaimed and the children who had been watching warily dashed down the bank and started clapping Lily and Abe on the back and celebrating. Pattie and Ted were first to get to Lily and hugged her tightly.

'You're never going away without me again!' Pattie told her.

'I missed you, Lily!' said Ted.

'And I missed you,' she said, crouching down and embracing him tightly. He hugged her back and then his face creased. 'Lily, I need a wee!'

Lily started to laugh, her face relaxing properly for the first time. 'Some things never change,' she said, catching Thomas's eye.

Thomas started to laugh too, feeling relief surge through him. His plan had worked. Lily and Abe were both free.

'Thanks,' Lily mouthed as if she could tell what he was thinking.

He shrugged like it was no big deal, but inside he felt like he was fizzing with happiness.

The general turned to Gran. 'We'll arrange for Abraham's travel home but he may need somewhere to stay for a while until it's safe to travel.'

'He can stay with us,' said Gran immediately. 'The more the merrier. That's right, isn't it, Thomas?'

He grinned, remembering how just a short while ago he hadn't even wanted the three evacuees to stay. 'Definitely!' he declared. His eyes met Abe's. 'We're all family now.'

CHAPTER TWENTY-FOUR

Lily felt her life over the next month was the happiest it had ever been – she still missed her mum but every week she and the others got a letter with a big heart drawn on the back. Listening to the grown-ups talking, she learned that the bombs were stopping and the war was coming to an end, which gave her hope that one day they'd be able to go back home and be a family again. In the meantime she made the most of her new wartime family – Abe, Thomas, Annie, Bobbie and Uncle Walter, when he was able to visit.

There were so many things to learn about and do – not just schoolwork but things like harvesting vegetables – pulling carrots and potatoes from the ground with the dark soil still clinging to them; picking the runner beans and the round peas in their fat green pods; and collecting the apples from the trees as the leaves started to change colour from green to russet, gold and brown.

They learned how to bake loaves of bread and Bobbie's rock cakes and hot, crisp Yorkshire puddings. On Mondays they helped with the washing, Wednesdays were mending days and Fridays were cleaning days. When they weren't helping out in the house or at school, they ran wild in the countryside, playing hide-and-seek, riding on an old bike, trying to catch fish in the river and rolling down the hills, yelling as they got faster and faster. Lily sometimes reflected with a smile how she had once thought there was too much countryside in Oakworth. Now she loved the rocky peaks, the patchwork of fields, the bubbling streams and the copses of ancient trees. Okay, the countryside couldn't block out the war completely – she remembered the German bomber only too well – but the rugged beauty and unchanging nature of the landscape made her feel sure that a time would come when the war would end and life would go on.

There was also the railway to visit. The junkyard became their playground and they loved to watch the trains steaming by – they even gave them all names. At the station Richard was always ready to make them a mug of tea and share any biscuits he had. The station master was less keen to see them at first – he hadn't forgotten the egg incident – but gradually even he started to thaw and he arranged for them to have a ride on one of the trains that steamed through the valley.

And there was Bobbie, always ready to give a smile and a hug. Lily would sometimes see her watching them, her face softening as though she was remembering another family and another time. She loved them all but it was Lily who her eyes rested on most frequently and Lily who she talked to in the evenings about when she'd been younger and had been a suffragette, fighting for women to have the right to vote. 'We won the battle but the war's not over yet,' she told her. 'It's young women like you, Lily, who will have to take up the fight when the war is over. You have so much passion, so much courage. You must use those things for good and to make the future better for everyone.'

'I will,' Lily promised.

Lily wrote down everything in her letters to her mum and when she put the letters in an envelope Annie would usually add a note of her own to Angela, their mum, telling her about various things that Lily had not thought to mention – Ted losing a tooth, Pattie having a haircut, Lily growing another inch.

Their lives were so full and fun that Lily felt like the summer would go on forever. But as the swathes of bracken that cloaked the steep slopes turned from green to brown and the swallows started to leave, heading for sunnier lands, a letter arrived for Abe, telling him that transport had been arranged for him to go home to New York. Lily didn't know whether to feel happy or sad. She was delighted for Abe – she knew he was longing to see his mum, or mom as he called her, but she also knew she was going to miss him a lot.

Uncle Walter drove them to the train station and handed Abe the leather suitcase that Bobbie had given to him. In it were packed all kinds of things – his clothes, a recipe for rock cakes from Bobbie, some comics that Thomas had given him, a piece of polished glass that Ted had found in the river, a new hanky that Pattie had embroidered with his initials and a wrapped-up razor that Lily had slipped in as a joke. Only unlike the last time she had taken a razor for him, this time she'd thought about what Thomas would do and had asked Annie if she could have it.

Chattering together, they all went through the ticket office and waited on the platform. After a few minutes, they heard the familiar huffing of a train and with a whistle and a scream of brakes it arrived in the station, squealing to a halt in clouds of smoke and a smell of fires. The doors began to open and people piled out.

'Take care, young man. Have a safe journey home,' Uncle Walter said to Abe.

Bobbie and Annie kissed him and then Pattie and Ted threw their arms round him. 'We'll miss you so much!' said Pattie, as Thomas stepped forward and rather awkwardly shook his hand.

'I hope you get back safely, Abe,' he said.

Abe shook his hand hard. 'Thanks, Tom.'

Lily wondered for a moment whether she should just shake hands too but as she met Abe's deep brown eyes, she forgot that idea and hugged him instead.

'Make sure you write me,' Abe told her, his voice muffled against her hair, his arms tight round her.

'I will, and you me,' she told him, her grip just as strong.

'You bet, and maybe when all this is over, I'll come back and visit you.'

'Or maybe I'll come to you,' Lily told him. She wasn't going to sit around waiting for any boy!

'Here's hoping,' he said, and with a grin he leaped on to the train. Shutting the door behind him, he opened the window and leaned out to wave goodbye. The guard walked along the platform, slamming doors shut and blowing his whistle.

The wheels started to turn and with an eruption of noise and clouds of steam, the train puffed out of the station. Abe hung out of the window, waving.

'He's going home,' said Pattie, taking Lily's hand. 'We need to be happy for him.'

'I am,' said Lily, blinking away her tears. She looked up at the craggy mountains. On the lower slopes the grass wasn't looking so green any more and leaves were falling from the trees. The land was settling down for its winter sleep. But it wouldn't sleep forever – a time of new growth would come.

And a time will come when I'll see Abe again, Lily thought determinedly. *I don't know how right now, but when this war is over I'll find a way.*

The thought of setting off on an American adventure made her smile and feel better about saying goodbye. She turned from waving at the vanishing train and froze. A brown-haired woman was hurrying along the platform from the other end, one hand on her hat, another carrying a suitcase.

'Lily! Oh, Lily!' she cried, her voice cutting through the platform noise. 'Pattie! Ted!'

'Mum?' Lily whispered in shock.

Annie squeezed her arm. 'Your mum told me she had

a few days' holiday. I thought you'd all like to see her, so I've invited her to stay.'

'Mummy!' shrieked Pattie. She hared down the platform to meet her with Ted but Lily overtook them both. A few blissful seconds later, she was in her mum's arms, breathing in her familiar perfume and feeling the weight of responsibility finally fall off her shoulders. Ted and Pattie cannoned into them and threw their arms round them both too.

Their mum was half crying and half laughing. 'Oh, my sweethearts,' she gasped out.

Standing with his own mum and gran, watching the ecstatic reunion of the Watts family, Thomas felt his heart fill with joy. He glanced up at his gran and saw a part-wistful, part-happy smile on her face. He wondered if she was thinking back to a time she had told him about when her father and younger brother had both been still alive, maybe even back to when she'd met her father at this very station after he'd been away a long time . . .

His mum squeezed his shoulder. 'It'll be your dad coming home next, Tom.'

Just that morning they'd had a letter from his dad in his prisoner-of-war camp. He'd sounded quite cheerful and he'd written of all the things he wanted to do when he came home – going for long walks and fishing trips with Thomas, taking his mum dancing, eating Bobbie's crumbles and pies.

Thomas felt a comforting glow of hope. 'It's going to be okay, isn't it, Mum?'

His mum pulled him close. 'I think we'll survive.'

'Surviving is undoubtedly important,' said Bobbie softly, her eyes on Lily, Pattie and Ted. 'But learning to live is what really matters.'

And as the last swallows of summer swooped above their heads and the shafts of autumn sun lit up the ancient landscape, Thomas looked at his gran and smiled.